HALF A DIRTY DOZEN

Skye saw them, six Ute warriors, surrounding Caroline, pulling at her dress, exposing her long beautiful legs, as she fought to keep the dress down.

The Trailsman couldn't use his gun—it would only give warning to other Indians nearby. His hand went to his throwing knife. He took aim at the Ute holding Caroline as another brave lifted her skirt still higher.

The blade went into the brave's sternum, shattering the bone as it penetrated to the hilt. The others stared frozen, transfixed by the sudden explosion of death. Fargo raced forward, his rifle held like a club. He whipped the barrel across the temple of the nearest Ute, and the Indian went down. Fargo bashed the butt into the throat of the next, and the Ute fell with a terrible, gargling sound from his smashed larynx.

Three down, and three left to kill—as the other braves closed in with murder on their minds and the odds on their side. . . .

THE
TRAILSMAN
188

MERCY
MANHUNT

by

Jon Sharpe ®

A SIGNET BOOK

SIGNET
Published by the Penguin Group
Penguin Books USA Inc., 375 Hudson Street,
New York, New York 10014, U.S.A.
Penguin Books Ltd, 27 Wrights Lane,
London W8 5TZ, England
Penguin Books Australia Ltd,
Ringwood, Victoria, Australia
Penguin Books Canada Ltd, 10 Alcorn Avenue,
Toronto, Ontario, Canada M4V 3B2
Penguin Books (N.Z.) Ltd, 182–190 Wairau Road,
Auckland 10, New Zealand

Penguin Books Ltd, Registered Offices:
Harmondsworth, Middlesex, England

First published by Signet, an imprint of Dutton Signet,
a division of Penguin Books USA Inc.

First Printing, August, 1997
10 9 8 7 6 5 4 3 2

The first chapter of this book originally appeared in *Sioux War Cry*,
the one hundred eighty-seventh volume in this series.

 REGISTERED TRADEMARK—MARCA REGISTRADA

Printed in Canada

The Trailsman

Beginnings . . . they bend the tree and they mark the man. Skye Fargo was born when he was eighteen. Terror was his midwife, vengeance his first cry. Killing spawned Skye Fargo, ruthless, cold-blooded murder. Out of the acrid smoke of gunpowder still hanging in the air, he rose, cried out a promise never forgotten.

The Trailsman they began to call him all across the West: searcher, scout, hunter, the man who could see where others only looked, his skills for hire but not his soul, the man who lived each day to the fullest, yet trailed each tomorrow. Skye Fargo, the Trailsman, and the seeker who could take the wildness of a land and the wanting of a woman and make them his own.

*1860, the Wyoming territory
north of Red Canyon, where death
rides a mission of mercy . . .*

1

"Damn!"

Skye Fargo spit the word out as he ducked and felt the razor nick his cheek. Crouched, the razor still in his hand, the sound of the shot rang in his ears. The shot had come from a distance, a stray rifle bullet, much of the power gone from it as it thudded into the tree six inches from him. But it still had enough force to knock the little mirror out of the crook in the branch where he had set it.

"Jesus, can't a man get a morning shave around here," he muttered as he peered across the stretch of open land. More shots erupted and then the wagon came into sight, canvas-topped, a driver whipping the team to go as fast as they could. Fargo saw the three riders pursuing the wagon appear, and then he saw five more following. The riders were quickly catching up to their quarry, all of them bent on sending a steady stream of rifle bullets at the fleeing wagon.

Fargo stayed crouched at the edge of the forest of hackberry where he had bedded down for the night. He watched the wagon driver swerve to try and avoid bullets and as he watched he saw a figure topple from the rear of the wagon. Two of the pursuers immediately poured bullets into it as they raced past. He frowned as he glimpsed two women inside the wagon when the canvas blew open at one side. The attackers were closing in on the wagon and Fargo put down the razor that was still in his hand. Wearing only trousers, he reached out to where his gunbelt hung on a branch and strapped it on as another figure fell from the careening wagon. Fargo rose and ran to where the Ovaro grazed nearby. There was no time to saddle up, he realized, and he pulled himself onto the magnificent black-and-white horse and went into an instant gallop.

Charging across the open land, he leaned forward in the saddle as he drew the big Colt, he aimed and fired it and saw the rider alongside the wagon topple from his horse. The riders immediately slowed as they peered across at him and Fargo fired again. Another of the men fell sideways from his horse. But the other pursuers had come up and Fargo ducked low as he saw the fusillade of bullets fired at him. He sent the pinto into a tight turn and streaked back to the stand of hackberry as bullets whistled past him. He reached the forest and plunged into the trees. He halted after he'd gone a dozen or so yards and leaped from the horse's back to land in a six-foot-high thick cluster of sweet fennel. Sinking down at once in the blue-green leaves of the weeds, he peered through the fine filaments and saw four horsemen reach the edge of the forest, pause, and split up into two groups of two each.

Two moved to his right, two to his left. They had seen where he had raced into the forest and planned to close in on him from both sides and he uttered a grim, silent oath. They moved carefully, he noted, and he glimpsed two more horsemen come to a halt just outside the tree-line; they stayed back and waited. Fargo's eyes narrowed. He knew he could easily take down at least one with his first shot, but that shot would tell them where he was, and they'd pour a hail of bullets into the fennel. The four men were walking their horses, bending low in the saddle, listening as they scanned the thick forest undergrowth. Fargo knew he couldn't just lay low. The four horsemen were working their way back and forth. They'd come onto him in minutes and his lips drew back as his mind raced. He had to strike first without drawing the instant burst of return fire. He needed a few precious seconds, enough to make them run not shoot.

Glancing at the big hackberry behind him, he half rose, holstered the Colt, and closed his hands around the lowest branch. Using all the power in his muscled arms and shoulders, he slowly lifted himself onto the branch, taking care not to disturb a leaf. He climbed onto the branch above and slid his long body around to the back of the tree trunk. His eyes went down to where the four horsemen were moving slowly toward each other, guns in hand. They were nearing the cluster of sweet fennel as Fargo drew the Colt and took aim. He counted off another few seconds and fired one shot first. The figure below and to his right seemed to jump in place in the saddle as the bullet thudded down through him, finally toppling from his horse. The others raised their guns, backed their horses. They frowned as they searched for the spot to return fire.

Their confusion took only seconds but they were the precious seconds of consternation Fargo needed. His next two shots sent two more of the attackers falling from their horses. The fourth man bent low in the saddle as he sent his horse racing from the forest. Fargo stayed in place, peering through the trees as the man joined the other two, and all three decided to leave, turning their horses and galloping across the open land. Fargo stayed in place until they were out of sight before he swung down out of the tree and stepped to where the three life-less forms lay silent and still. He went through each man's pockets, found coins, some paper money, keys, and tobacco, nothing that identified anyone. Lips pursed, Fargo called the Ovaro, swung onto the horse and again rode bareback out of the forest.

He passed the spot where he had been shaving, his clothes and saddle still on the ground as he rode past. Out on the open land he picked up the wagon tracks where the driver had fled west, followed the wheel marks around a curved line of serviceberry, and finally saw the wagon halted beside an arch of volcanic rock. The driver saw his approach and lowered the rifle he held in his hands. "The horses gave out," the man said as Fargo rode to a halt, a square face with a neatly cropped gray beard and bright, blue eyes surrounded by a visage of crinkles and lines. "Where are they?" the driver asked.

"Gone," Fargo said and saw the two women push their heads out of the wagon, both their middle-aged faces drawn tight.

"We'd all be dead if you hadn't come along, mister," the driver said.

"Name's Fargo . . . Skye Fargo," the Trailsman said.

"Ben Smith," the man said and Fargo guessed he had some seventy years on him.

"Why were they after you?" Fargo asked.

"Damned if I know," Ben Smith said and looked at the two women. The taller of the two spoke up, her eyes still holding disbelief and shock.

"No reason for it, no reason at all. We didn't know them. They just came at us and started shooting. I'm Grace Tumbley and this is my friend Joan Ladden. My husband Sam and I organized the trip. They killed him with their first shot. He was riding alongside the wagon. We hired Ben on as driver."

"I'm guessing they were a passel of stinking dry-gulchers looking to rob us," Ben Smith said.

"Most wagons don't carry enough money to be good targets for robbing," Fargo said.

"That's right, but some do," Ben said, and Fargo conceded the point with a half shrug.

"You tell people where you were going?" he asked Grace Tumbley.

"Of course. That's just natural when you're equipping a wagon," she said.

"Where were you headed?" Fargo questioned.

"Northwest, to find our way past the Caribou range and keep going. We met in Green Springs and planned everything together."

"Green Springs? That's where I'm headed," Fargo said. "But one wagon going into the northwest country, that wasn't too smart an idea."

"Told them that," Ben Smith put in.

"There were four of us, plus Ben and two men who paid to come along," Grace Tumbley said. "We all decided that a single wagon wouldn't draw much attention from anyone, including Indians."

"Guess you decided wrong," Fargo said and let his eyes go to the wagon. He saw that it was a Texas wagon outfitted with top bows for a canvas roof and sides. Not as rugged as a Conestoga, it was nonetheless a fairly durable wagon, though the country they had headed for would give any wagon a terrible test. "Think your horses are ready to move?" he asked and the man nodded. "Turn around, go back to Green Springs. I'll get my things and come help you with what has to be done," Fargo said.

Ben Smith nodded grimly and Fargo put the Ovaro into a fast canter and rode back across the open land to the hackberry forest. He dismounted, took a few minutes to put his pocket mirror back in place and finish shaving before he put the saddle on the horse. Setting out again, he found Ben Smith and the wagon halted and he dismounted to help tie the slain figures onto the backs of their horses. When the grim business was finished, he rode beside the wagon and heard the two women crying softly inside. "This is sure to be all over town a few minutes after we get there," Ben Smith said.

"Why?" Fargo asked.

"Green Springs has always been a kind-of starting place for wagon trains going north, west, even south. They take pride in being a good-luck place to start from. There's never been an attack like this," Ben said.

"Another thing that makes me wonder about it being a plain old robbery," Fargo said.

"You've another reason you're thinking about?" the old driver said.

"No, unfortunately," Fargo admitted.

"What brings you to Green Springs, Fargo?" Ben asked.

"Somebody asked me to meet them there," Fargo said.

"You're the one they call the Trailsman," the old driver said and Fargo shot him a glance of surprise. "Put it together soon as I had a moment's breather." Ben laughed. "Your name and that Ovaro. You've a reputation, Fargo. I've driven for enough people to have heard it. You going to break trail for somebody?"

"Truth is, I'm not sure but it's likely," Fargo said as the buildings of the town came into view. Green Springs turned out to be larger than he'd expected, Main Street wider, more buildings, more people, more bustle, more wagons. Most of them, he noted, were either Conestogas or smaller, light one-horse farm wagons. Ben Smith drew to a halt in front of a building with green-shaded windows and no name. "Undertaker's office?" Fargo asked, and he nodded.

"Thanks again for keeping a few of us alive," the old driver said.

"What'll the women do?" Fargo asked.

"Go back where they came from, I expect."

"And you?"

"People are always asking me to drive for them. I've a reputation of my own," he said with a touch of pride.

"Bet you do. Good luck, old-timer," Fargo said and moved the Ovaro on. He'd reached the center of town when he drew up before the small building with the sign SHERIFF on the window. Dismounting, he went inside where two men looked up from a single desk, one wearing a sheriff's badge on a body with thirty pounds too much on it. "Bill Delbard?" Fargo asked, and the man nodded. "Skye Fargo," the Trailsman said. The man's eyes widened as he rose.

"Sit down, please. We've been waiting for you," the sheriff said. "We weren't sure if you'd reached Hank's place?"

"I did and he told me you were waiting," Fargo said.

"Get Caroline," the sheriff said to the other man, who quickly strode from the office. "It's Caroline Sanders who wants to see you. She got in touch with me and I'd heard you were bringing a big herd in to Hank Bowers, so I got a message to him."

"I almost didn't make it," Fargo said and told the sheriff about the attack on the wagon.

"Good God," the sheriff said when Fargo finished. "That's a new one out here."

"So Ben Smith said."

"Glad he came through. He's been driving trains out of here for years, mostly going into the Southwest, though. He's a good old codger," the sheriff said as the door opened and a young woman strode into the office. She was tall and slender with a small waist inside a dark blue jacket that allowed only the slightest swell of breasts.

"Thank heavens you're here," she said to Fargo. "I'm Caroline Sanders. I asked the sheriff to find you for me." She extended a hand and he felt a firm handshake and his eyes took in very light yellow hair worn short, the color of bleached hay. Pale skin, light blue eyes, even her lips a pale pink, at first glance a delicate face, the coloring weak, almost washed out but the features strong, a straight nose, firm jaw, and strong cheekbones. A longer glance showed that the pale blue eyes almost hid a cool, self-contained assurance. Caroline Sanders was an uncommonly attractive set of mixtures, he decided. She sat down across from him and he glimpsed a long, slender calf.

"Hank Bowers said you sounded desperate," Fargo remarked.

"I am," Caroline Sanders said, leaning forward in her chair. "I need you for a mission of mercy. There's a wagon train of people with young children included who might be in danger of dying a terrible death. I've been working for Doc Dodson here in Green Springs for two years. Recently, he was hired to go on this wagon train because two of the women were close to giving birth."

"He left Green Springs on its own to do this?" Fargo frowned.

"They offered a good deal of money he said he would use to buy a lot of medicine for use in town. That's the kind of man Dr. Dodson is. Besides, he wasn't going the whole way with the wagons, just long enough for the women to give birth. Then he planned to ride back at once on his own," Caroline said. "He felt I could handle things until then."

"Are you a nurse?" Fargo questioned.

"Not yet. I've been training under Dr. Dodson," Caroline said, then reached into her pocket and handed Fargo a letter. She sat back and waited as he began to read the straight, strong handwriting.

Dear Caroline,

I am dispatching this by a special messenger. I have become increasingly disturbed by certain things I've observed. I fear there may be smallpox on the train. You, of course, know what this means if it is so. The only one I've mentioned it to is Frank Turner, as he heads the train. As I am not sure, we decided it would be wrong to alarm the entire train and perhaps cause unnecessary panic and perhaps conflict. But if I am right, you know how deadly this plague can be.

In the office cabinet there is enough serum to vaccinate everyone on the train. But time is everything. They must be vaccinated before there is an outbreak. You must get the serum to me before that happens and it is too late. You know how quickly this terrible plague can erupt.

Here is our route so far. We have traveled west. I wish I had taken the time to note landmarks. I can only recall a tall rock formation of arches and windows, a long forest of gambel oak, and a huge field of columbine, plus innumerable rivers and valleys and mountains. It is Frank Turner's plan to cross the Green River, follow the west shore, and then turn west again to try and find Bear Lake. Then he plans to skirt the Wasatch Range into Idaho, go northwest to the Snake River Plateau, and perhaps hook up with the Oregon trail there.

But so far we have only gone a small way and I hope you can catch up to me soon. I pray to God I am wrong in my fears but I dare not take that chance. Please hurry, my dear Caroline.

Dr. Dodson

Caroline spoke the moment Fargo lowered the letter. "I knew I'd never be able to pick up their trail so I asked the sheriff for help. He told me you were the very best and that you were expected at Hank Bowers'. I've been biting my nails down waiting. I need your help. All those people need your help. You'll be paid for an act of mercy."

"The serum is in bottles?" Fargo questioned.

"Inside boxes," Caroline answered. "I've a wagon I bought at Schneider's wagon shop to carry them." Fargo's lips pursed as he looked down at the letter again. "What is it?" Caroline asked.

"This is a damn fool way to take a wagon train," he said. "I wouldn't be sure they can make it, plague or no plague."

"Why not?"

"I'll give you four quick reasons: the Shoshoni, Ute, Arapaho, and Kiowa. They all prowl that territory," Fargo said.

"I understand there are some small communities and way stations along the way," she said.

"Small communities have a way of being massacred and way stations a way of being burned down," he said.

"You saying we can't find the train?" she asked.

He ignored the assumption in the word *we.* "I'm saying it's damn unlikely. It's a trail almost a month old now, maybe covered over by rain, wind, and new grass. Then, one wagon traveling alone is easy pickings."

"I've hired six men to go along for protection," she said.

"Six?" He snorted. "Twenty might mean something."

"I couldn't afford twenty," Caroline snapped back. "I'm sure you've ridden trail through dangerous country before," she said with a touch of asperity.

"I try to keep the odds down," he said.

"How?"

"By not following fools," he said and saw her lips tighten. The sheriff rose and started from the office.

"I'll leave you two to work this out," he said and hurried outside. Fargo saw Caroline's eyes were on him with a penetrating coolness.

"It's really quite simple. I have to reach those wagons and you have to help me," she said, more command than plea in her tone, and he noted the upward tilt of her chin.

"You've got something a little wrong there, honey," he said very quietly. "I'll help you, but because I want to, not because I have to."

She waited a moment. "Yes, of course," she said, concession without retreat. The pale delicacy of her definitely had another dimension, he decided. "Then we have an agreement?" she said.

"Yes," he said. She took a roll of bills from her jacket pocket and handed them to him.

"In advance," she said, and he nodded. "The wagon's waiting for me. I just have to pick it up, load it, and get in touch with Burt Hobbs. He's one of the men I hired. I'll be ready to roll by ten in the morning. We'll meet at

Doc Dodson's building, the small white one up the street. I have living quarters there." She rose, a graceful, fluid movement, and he went outside with her, where night had blanketed the town. "Where will you stay tonight?" she asked.

"Maybe in town. Anyplace to stay here?" he said.

Her pale blue eyes surveyed him for a long moment. "Go to the Rest Inn, east end of town. You'll get a good sleep there." She paused again for a moment. "I know you'll find those wagons. You see, I've more confidence in you than you do," she said.

"Thanks," he said laconically. Being confident was one thing. Being naive was another, he commented silently as he watched her hurry away, slender tallness held very straight. Prim, he thought, then changed it to aloof. He pulled himself onto the Ovaro and slowly walked the horse down Main Street, finally halting before an old, two-story frame house with filigreed woodwork on the outside and a small sign over the door. He dismounted and went inside and saw a large sitting room with a small front desk to one side. Four old ladies in the room looked up at him. They were all seated on worn sofas. Two stooped men, both with canes, moved gingerly across the floor. Two wizened old ladies were huddled under shawls over a checkerboard. A slow-moving little man that Fargo guessed weighed some ninety pounds rose from behind the front desk.

"Want a room, young feller?" he asked.

"Maybe later, thanks," Fargo said. "Be back if I do."

"Not after ten. We don't take any guests after ten," the man said.

"Got it," Fargo said as he returned to the Ovaro. He swung onto the horse again and decided his bedroll under a tree would be much preferable. It wasn't that the

Rest Inn's guests were octogenarian, they were museum pieces, the place itself tomblike, fit only for a good sleep, he murmured, recalling Caroline's words. Riding back along Main Street, he slowed when he reached an oblong square of yellow light coming from a noisy building. He didn't need the sign to tell him it was the town saloon, but he frowned at the sign next to it that read BED AND BOARD.

He tethered the Ovaro and went inside to find a typical saloon, sawdust-covered floor and a long bar, already half full of customers. A large-busted woman in a black gown greeted him with a smile that just managed not to be mechanical. "Room for the night?" Fargo asked.

"It's done," she said. "Give me your name, big man."

"Skye Fargo," he said. She wrote in a small ledger on a table behind her and handed him a large key.

"Two dollars," she said. "I'm Clora. Just a room?"

"A bourbon and something to eat," Fargo said.

"Beef stew is real good tonight. Find yourself a table. I'll have Dolly serve you. She's not a girl I let wait on the average customer, but you don't look like there's anything average about you," the woman said.

He let his eyes stay on her and decided she wasn't giving him a stock line. "Thanks," he said and made his way to a small table in a corner of the room. He relaxed with a sigh, glad he'd chosen not to stay at the Rest Inn. It had been a long, hard haul to Hank Bowers and he didn't fancy spending the night in a museum. Caroline Sanders obviously had no idea what a tired, thirsty man needed to relax. A young woman appeared with his bourbon and he took in a surprisingly fresh, open face without the hardness of most saloon girls. Her low-cut black waitress outfit showed a full, high pair of breasts that pushed up over the top of the neckline.

"Bourbon's on the house. Our way of welcoming a new customer," she said. "I'm Dolly."

"You don't care that I won't be around long?" Fargo smiled.

"You might come back, they figure," Dolly said.

"How do you figure?" he asked, and Dolly's brown eyes took in his muscled physique. "Hope you do," she said. "We don't get many real good-looking men in here." She waltzed off, not waiting for him to answer. He ordered a second bourbon when she returned with his meal and he enjoyed the open-faced freshness of her. She showed none of the jaded artifices of most saloon girls. He ate slowly. The stew was tasty, and he watched Dolly as she returned to lean both palms on the table. "We've satisfied part of you," she said. "Let me know if there's anything more you'd like satisfied." Again, no leer in her voice at all, no artificial suggestiveness, just an appealing honesty. His thoughts flicked to the trip that lay ahead, a mission of mercy that could well be a mission to disaster.

He took the key from his pocket, looked at it. "Room four," he said.

"Ground floor next door," Dolly said.

"Give me ten minutes to stable my horse," he said, and she nodded with a private little smile. He hurried from the saloon, found the public stable he had noted earlier, and secured a nice roomy corner stall for the Ovaro. He strode back to find the room. In it was a lamp, a chair, and a double bed, and a washstand and a pitcher of water. No frills, but clean, and he undressed down to his shorts, hung the gunbelt on the bedpost, and opened the door at the knock. Dolly slid into the room, her eyes instantly moving across the contours of his smoothly muscled body, more than approval in her perusal. She unsnapped catches, opened buttons, and the dress fell away as he lowered himself onto the bed. Dolly's full breasts were not as full as they had seemed in the dress, yet they were attractive enough. Her waist a little thick, legs a trifle heavy in the thighs, yet she came to him with an eagerness that was unforced.

Her body came against him and she gave a little cry of delight and he felt the dark triangle rub against his groin. "This is going to be my lucky night," Dolly murmured.

"Our lucky night, I'm thinking," Fargo said, and she gave a happy little chuckle and brought her breasts up to his face. He was just beginning to taste one when the sharp knock at the door shattered the moment. Dolly drew back, frowning, and Fargo's brow furrowed as the knock came again, sharper this time. Dolly was still half over him when the door was pushed open. Fargo's jaw dropped as Caroline strode in, her jaw set.

"Get out," she hissed at Dolly, picking up the dress and throwing it at her. "Now, out," she snapped. Dolly rose, holding the dress in front of her as she hurried past Caroline and out of the room.

"What the hell do you think you're doing?" Fargo said from the bed, swinging long legs over the side.

"Protecting my interests," she shot back.

"What I do is my business." Fargo frowned.

"Not if it affects how you do your job. We have to make time starting tomorrow. I don't want you nursing a hangover from too much bourbon and half asleep from too much screwing," Caroline said stiffly.

"You've got your goddamn nerve," Fargo protested.

"It's my prerogative. You're working for me, now," she returned haughtily.

"I can fix that," he said, rising and pulling the roll of bills from his jacket. "Here's your damn money."

"You can't do that," she said, unmoved.

"I just did, dammit," he said.

"We made an agreement. You don't go back on your word. That seems to be common knowledge," she said with a note of triumph.

"How do you know that?" Fargo frowned.

"When I heard how good you are as a trailsman, I asked more and heard how good you are with the ladies and bourbon," she said. "I thought it best to rein in that part of you."

He felt the astonishment flooding through him. "That damn inn . . . that's why you sent me there to sleep," he muttered.

"It offered no temptations. When I checked back and found you weren't there I knew where you'd be," she said.

"You're a piece of work, aren't you?" Fargo said.

"Now, you can get a good night's sleep. That's all I care about," she said, but he saw her eyes move across his near-naked muscled body.

"I might just go back and find me another girl," he said.

"They won't service you," Caroline said smugly.

"Why the hell not?" he bristled.

"I told them I was counting on you to bring Doc Dodson back. The doc's important to everyone in town, saloon girls, too," she said.

He stared at her. Pale ice. Delicate steel. Through his anger, he felt a grudging admiration for her. "Get the hell out of here," he growled.

"Good night, Fargo," she said as she strode from the room, closing the door gently after her. He lay back on the bed, turned off the lamp, and promised himself to conclude this mission of mercy as quickly as he could.

2

He did get a good sleep, Fargo admitted to himself with a touch of surprise, considering how angry he'd been at Caroline's high-handed ways. Dressed, he retrieved the Ovaro from the public stable and found his way to the white frame house, where he had another moment of surprise when he found Ben Smith talking to Caroline.

"Didn't expect to see you again, old-timer," Fargo said.

"You'll be seeing more of me. Miss Caroline's hired me on," Ben Smith said.

"I know I'll need an experienced driver and that's certainly not me. I asked around and found Ben," Caroline said. She still wore the coolly efficient-looking dark blue jacket and her face seemed even more delicately colored in the morning sunlight.

"I don't see any wagon," Fargo said as he glanced about and saw Caroline's face tighten.

"Mr. Schneider informed me that he found a crack in the axle of my wagon and he has to put on a new skein. It won't be ready till tomorrow. Needless to say, I'm terribly upset but there's nothing to do but wait," she said.

"We'll have to make the best of it," Fargo said blandly. Caroline's eyes narrowed as she caught the unsaid in his remark.

"Not the way you're thinking," she said. He turned and shrugged as a wagon rolled up to a halt and he took in a big hay wagon that had been converted into a semi-Conestoga with added upright slats and a long canvas top. Two men rode alongside it, he noted, and two young women sat up front on the high, upward curve of the prow of the wagon. One held the reins of a team of powerful, heavy-legged Percherons. She had a round face, short, brown curls tinged with red. Fargo guessed her to be nudging thirty, a pretty-enough face but already showing lines in it. The woman beside her was perhaps a little younger but her face also a little harder with too much makeup on her eyes. One side of the canvas lifted and Fargo saw a third young woman and a young, owlish-looking man inside.

"You Caroline Sanders?" the woman with the reins asked Caroline.

"That's right." Caroline nodded.

"You're going after the Turner wagon train," the young woman said.

"I am," Caroline said.

"So are we. I'm Holly Crater," the young woman said. "We came to join up with you."

Fargo interrupted as he turned to Caroline. "How many people did you tell?" he asked.

"It's all over town," the young woman said.

"Jesus," Fargo grunted.

"Of course I told people, especially when I was looking for a trailsman," Caroline said to Fargo.

"We heard you hired the very best one," Holly Crater said and turned an appraising glance at Fargo. "Would that be you?" she asked. "You look like you'd be pretty good at anything."

26

"Thanks. I try," Fargo said evenly. "Name's Fargo . . . Skye Fargo."

"Look here, Miss . . ." Caroline broke in.

"Holly Crater."

"I'm not adding anyone," Caroline said. "We'll be traveling alone. One wagon will make much better time than two. Certainly that cumbersome old thing you have would slow us down. It's out of the question."

"We're not asking for a free ride. We'll pay half the cost of hiring Fargo, more, if you want," Holly Crater said.

"I'm sorry, the answer is still no," Caroline said. "Just who are you, anyway, and why do you want to reach the Turner wagons?"

"We all have friends or relatives on those wagons. When we heard there might be smallpox on the train we decided to try and reach them to do anything we could," Holly Crater said and gestured to the woman beside her. "This is my friend Randi Howell. Terry Jones is inside. Our good friend Lila Tomkins is with the Turner wagon train. We're schoolteachers. We want to open a school. Lila went ahead to find the right place for us." Fargo let his gaze hold on Holly Crater and the other woman, but he stayed silent as Caroline questioned again.

"And the rest of you?" she asked.

Holly Crater gestured to the man nearest on a brown gelding. Fargo guessed him to be pushing fifty, with a face of small, tight features, brown hair slicked down flat on his head, and wearing a vest under a well-cut jacket. "Harry Adamson," she said.

"My lifelong friend Donald Burton is on the Turner wagons," Harry Adamson said.

Holly's eyes nodded at the other man. "Herb Baxter," she said, and Fargo took in a thin, balding man with a pinched face and unhappy eyes, a lean body that fit the face.

"Aran Stillman and Bettie are on that wagon train. They're very close to me," the man said and Fargo's eyes went to the rear of the wagon as the younger man swung into sight. Sandy, unruly hair tumbled over his forehead and horn-rimmed spectacles added to his owlish appearance.

"Ernie Alden," he said in a somewhat high voice. "My cousin Orrin Dodge is with the Turner wagons. I want to be with him if he's in trouble."

"You see, we all want to reach those wagons, to be with the people we care about. It's very important to all of us for our own reasons," Holly Crater said.

"You'll have to go on your own," Caroline said stiffly. "The serum I'm taking is the only thing that will save those people if there is an epidemic. That's the only thing they'll need."

"It's not fair to push us aside. These are our friends and relatives," Holly Crater protested.

"I'm sorry, the answer is still no. I'm not taking you or anyone else along. I'm going with one wagon and making time," Caroline said.

"There are lots of ways we'd be of help," Holly Crater said.

"I told you, that serum is the only help that will count," Caroline said, dismissing further argument as she turned to Fargo. "Mr. Schneider said he'd have a definite time when the wagon will be ready. I should know today, I'd guess sometime later this afternoon. Stop by then." He nodded and Caroline hurried into the house.

"Shit," Randi Howell hissed from beside Holly. "She's a real bitch."

"That's enough, Randi," Holly Crater said sharply, and then, her tone softening, "Everyone has their own way of looking at things." She turned her eyes to Fargo. Her short brown curls helped give her round-cheeked face a softness that let her look younger than she was, he decided. She wore a denim jacket that didn't stop the swell of full breasts. "As you can see, we're all under a terrible strain," Holly Crater said to Fargo. "Where can we talk privately?"

"Seems I'll be staying another night in the rooms alongside the saloon," Fargo said. "And you?"

"Camping outside of town. I'll come visit you," she said, snapped the reins, and the big Percherons leaned forward, the heavy wagon following. Fargo watched the riders and wagon move away until Ben Smith cut into his thoughts.

"What are you thinking, Fargo?" the old driver asked.

"I'm thinking they're not schoolteachers," Fargo said as he led the Ovaro down the street.

"How do you know?"

"I don't. Just a feeling," Fargo said.

"Maybe they're just different than the average schoolteacher," Ben Smith ventured.

"Maybe," Fargo said as he halted before the public stable. "I'm going to give my horse a thorough grooming. I like a horse freshly groomed before we hit the trail."

"See you tomorrow," Ben said and walked away on slightly bowed legs, Fargo noticed. Leading the Ovaro into the stable, Fargo made use of a bucket of water and large rubbing towels they supplied, taking the rest of the grooming tools from a pouch on his saddle. He started with the dandy brush for heavy dirt and caked sweat, then the body brush for scruff from the horse's mane and tail. A good stable sponge cleaned eyes, nostrils, and lips, then the sweat scraper on the coat, and after that the big, soft cloths for a final polishing. He went to the hoof pick then for removing small stones and grit from the hooves. He shed his shirt soon after he started and worked slowly and lovingly until the Ovaro glistened and gleamed, its fore-and-hindquarters a shining black, its midsection pure white. The day was nearing an end when he finished.

"He'll be here another night," he said to the stable-man. "Give him the same big corner stall."

"Yes, sir. He's special," the man said with the experienced eye of one who knows horses.

"Very," Fargo agreed, and giving the Ovaro a final pat he strode from the stable and walked to the saloon, to find Holly Crater there.

"Decided to visit early," she said and followed him to the room. "You wanted to talk," he said as Holly lowered herself to the edge of the bed. The denim jacket came from her shoulders and she wore a pale yellow shirt underneath that fitted tight around full, round breasts, the two points pushing into the fabric. "Let me guess." Fargo smiled. "You want me to convince Caroline Sanders to let you come along."

Holly Crater sighed with a sheepish smile. "Didn't take much guessing, did it?" she murmured. "It's so important to all of us. We can't just sit around waiting and wondering. We're sick with worry now. This way we'll at least feel we're trying to do something."

Fargo's lips pursed. "She's right, you know, about one wagon making better time," he said.

"But we've other things to offer. If there's trouble, any kind of trouble, it'd be good to have help, more bodies, more guns, more anything," Holly said. "And we wouldn't slow you down that much. Besides, they're our friends and relatives. We have a right to see to them."

"Maybe, but it's not my call, Holly," Fargo said.

"She'd listen to you. I'm sure you could convince her, point out how we'd be good to have along," Holly said. She sat up very straight and the pale yellow shirt drew tight across her breasts. Her hand went to the top buttons of the blouse. "Talk is just talk. I can do better," Holly said.

"I'll bet you can," Fargo said.

Her hand opened the top buttons of the blouse and he immediately saw the full swell of her breasts push outward. "This what you teach in school?" he asked mildly.

"I'm not in school now," she said and another button came open.

Fargo's smile was rueful. "I'm not up for sale, honey," he said.

"Didn't say you were," Holly replied. "But a man can be persuaded."

"Don't sugar your words. You mean bought," he said. "Sorry, I don't sell out, not for hard cash or soft pussy. They've both been tried before."

She blinked and her hand halted at the next button. "I'm sorry, I didn't see it as you selling out. I didn't mean it that way," she said, her found face suddenly contrite. She offered a rueful half smile. "Bad move, wasn't it?" she murmured.

"With somebody else, maybe not. With me, yes," he said.

Her rueful half smile stayed. "This was my idea but I guess now you know how much it means to all of us," she said as she buttoned the pale yellow shirt. She rose and came to him. "Sorry I made such a fool of myself," she said. She was appealing in her rush of contriteness, and he felt a wave of sympathy sweep over him, perhaps unwarranted, he realized, yet it pulled at him. She had become intriguing in a variety of ways.

"I'll talk to Caroline Sanders again. I'll give it a try for you but I'll tell you now I don't expect she'll listen," he said.

Holly Crater's arms flew around his neck, her face brightening instantly, and he felt the warm softness of her breasts touch his chest. "That's all I can ask. Everyone will be grateful," she said. She brought her lips to his, an impulsive motion, a quick kiss, and she put only warm gratefulness in it. "Thanks, really thanks," she said, pulling back, her eyes moving across his chiseled features. "I'm sort of glad you can't be bought," she said reflectively. "But I'm sure buying would have been great."

"Maybe there'll be a better time, a better reason," he said and walked from the room with her.

"How do I find out what she says?" Holly asked.

"Come by later," he said, and she hurried away, hips swinging. Smiling, he went into the street, where dusk had begun to descend. He walked to the white frame house and Caroline came to the door at his knock. She had taken off the blue jacket and a white blouse rested lightly on a modest bustline, perhaps a little long, yet it seemed to fit perfectly with her slender, narrow-waisted torso.

"First thing in the morning. I'd like to get as early a start as possible," she said.

"Good enough. I've been thinking about that other wagon. There might be some good in taking them along," he said casually.

"Such as?" She frowned.

"A backup wagon might be insurance. Suppose you

have a breakdown, a wheel goes, you'd have another wagon to carry the serum," he suggested.

"I'd give a few bottles to Burt Hobbs and each of his men to carry," she said.

"They're going to fight off a Shoshoni war party while carrying the serum?" Fargo questioned.

"I'm hoping neither of those things will be happening," Caroline said.

"Don't count on it," Fargo said. "Extra hands, extra guns, they could come in handy."

"I won't be slowed down by another wagon, certainly not that lumbering old thing. Besides, if smallpox has broken out they'll only be in the way, more of a hindrance than a help. Doc Dodson always made sure not to have friends and relatives around when there was a crisis. No, I'll have none of it," Caroline said and Fargo nodded. She wasn't about to change her mind, he saw, and he was satisfied with the logic of her decisions. He turned to go, paused, and slid a smile at her. "You going to come checking again tonight?" he asked.

"There'll be no need," she said, and he felt an eyebrow lift. She indulged in overconfidence, he grunted silently as she closed the door. Night dropped over the town and he strolled down the street, suddenly aware that hunger pushed at him and he turned in at the saloon. The big-busted Clora wasn't at the door and he found a table for himself. He'd only been seated a minute when Dolly appeared.

"I'm sorry about last night. She scared me," Dolly said.

"Forget it. We can take up where we left off tonight," Fargo said.

Dolly's face showed instant discomfort. "No," she said, almost whispering the word. "Nobody will."

He frowned at her. "Caroline Sanders again? She have that damn much influence?"

"She talked to Clora but it's not her. It's Doc Dodson. We all need him. He'd always looked after us, treated us with respect. She said you're the key to reaching him. Nobody here will do anything to affect that."

Fargo let a wry grunt escape him, Caroline's self-confidence explained. It hadn't been at all misplaced. "I take a bourbon and a hot meal are okay?" he growled peevishly.

"On the house," Dolly said and hurried away. She returned soon and he lingered over the bourbon, watched the saloon fill with customers, and finally finished the meal and rose. Dolly was beside him at once. "When you come back. Promise," she said, her hand squeezing his arm.

"Just might take you up on that," he said, giving her a pat and walking into the darkness outside. He went to the room, undressed, and stretched out on the bed, the lamp turned down low. He was slowly drifting off to sleep when the knock came at the door, polite and almost delicate. He drew on his underwear and opened the door to see Holly Crater there, the denim jacket around her shoulders.

"You said to come by later," she reminded him.

"So I did," he said, letting her in, and he saw her eyes roam across his near-naked smoothly muscled body. He reached to draw on his jeans and she halted him.

"That's all right," she said. "Just tell me what she said."

"She said no," he answered. "You're disappointed, of course."

"I'd hoped she might listen to you."

"I gave it a good try, believe me," he said.

34

"I believe you," Holly nodded, her eyes again moving across his powerful physique. "I'd like to thank you for that," she said, slipping off the denim jacket. The pale yellow blouse still stretched tight across her breasts. "No buying, no asking, no strings. Nothing. You won't be selling out."

"Not even a hope for another time?" He smiled.

"Maybe down deep somewhere. I can't really answer that," Holly said. "I'm not much for wondering about tomorrows. I'm not much for turning away from today, either," she said, and her fingers went to the buttons of the blouse.

"Me neither," he said, and her fingers moved more quickly. He watched as the pale yellow blouse came off and two full well-shaped breasts seemed to cascade forward with newfound freedom, each tipped with a dark red nipple and a large areola. She slid her skirt down, stepped toward him beautifully naked, and he took in a body a little thick around the middle, a rounded belly and below it tiny folds just over the black, bushy triangle. Her thighs were also a little thick, yet she exuded an energetic sensuality that made everything else unimportant.

She came to him, wrapped her arms around him, and her body pressed itself tight to his, breasts soft and cushiony against him. "Jesus," Holly Crater murmured. "You're a man to remember."

"Let's find out," Fargo said as he pulled her onto the bed, shed his drawers and Holly's breasts were into his face at once, the dull-red nipples seeming to find their own way to his mouth. He caressed first one, then the other, took each deeply into his mouth and Holly gave a tiny groan of utter pleasure. He felt her hands move down between his muscled thighs, find him and she gasped a sharp cry.

"Oh, God, oh, Jesus, yes . . . oh, yes," she said, and her fingers closed around him, stroking, caressing, and he felt her hips turn upward. He stroked the fleshy thighs, and her legs came open at once, staying open as she gave a little moan and her torso half twisted. His hand moved over the tiny little folds just above her pubic mound, pushing into the thick, black bush. Holly's legs lifted her torso upward, the body uttering its own silent entreaties. He moved his hand downward, cupping the softness of her, and she cried out, a long, deep moan, and her torso quivered with wanting. But he refused to indulge pleasure so quickly and he toyed with her, small strokes along the edges of the moist lips, a touch moving deeper, drawing back, then forward again. "Damn, oh, damn . . . more, more," Holly gasped out and her hips lifted again.

Patience, subtlety, they were not part of her, he realized, and as her hand closed around him again, he moved, letting her guide him into the warm dampness of her. She cried out, a long, sighing sound that combined utter satisfaction and utter abandon as he filled her. Her fleshy thighs closed around him, her body pumping with an energetic fury, lifting upward, dropping back, then upward, back and forth, up and down, hurrying faster each time. No savoring for Holly, no slow delights, only a furious pubic rush to satisfaction. He matched her desires, fell into her rhythm, answered her every heaving thrust.

Her cries rose and she pulled his face down to her breasts, all of her suddenly quivering. Then her body shook violently and she screamed out the words, "Yes, yes, yes . . . damn, damn . . . now, now, oh, Jesus now, yes . . ." and her thighs lifted, sliding against his hips as she became a paroxysm of quaking, jouncing flesh. Her long, almost angry scream gave the ultimate message and he let himself explode with her as she twitched and writhed against him, holding him to her with legs, arms, vulva, mouth, every part of her clasped around him. When the penultimate moment of ecstasy passed, she fell away from him, arms flopping outward, legs sliding downward, her shaking, quivering contractions vanishing at once and a deep sigh came from her. "God, wonderful . . . wonderful," she breathed. "But then I knew it would be with you."

"How'd you know?" he asked.

"A feeling inside," she said, pushing up on the bed and reluctantly reaching for her clothes. "Wish I didn't have to go, but the others are waiting to hear."

He watched her dress, the full breasts disappearing behind the pale yellow blouse. "Do I go to the head of the class?" he asked.

"You sure do," she said, brushing his cheek with her lips and hurrying from the room. He stared at where she had been, seeing her in his mind, and a speculative half smile touched his lips. He rose, slid the bolt on the door, and returned to the bed, turning out the lamp and letting the darkness draw sleep around him. But only utter exhaustion brought him the sleep of most men. Sleep to Fargo was the sleep of the cougar, the wolf, and the deer, a small, silent part of him always awake, subconsciously alert to feel the presence of danger, to pick up the step of an enemy. He had slept perhaps an hour when the sliding, scraping sound woke him, hardly a noise at all, yet enough. His eyes snapped open but he lay motionless.

The faint sound came again, the window being inches open. Fargo's eyes went to where the holster hung on the bedpost, not close enough to reach without moving. His eyes went to the window again. It was half open now, a faint shaft of moonlight coming in, along with the man who climbed through, legs swinging in first. The man turned to the bed and Fargo saw the glint of the moonlight on the blade of a knife. Pressing his arms on the bed, he gathered the muscles of his shoulders and arms and shot himself upward in a twisting leap. He heard the man's oath and felt the knife graze his shoulder. He heard his own curse as his hand slipped from the gunbelt and he hit the floor. He twisted around and saw the figure diving down at him, knife upraised in one hand.

He managed to pull his head to the left and the knife touched his ear as it slammed down, the point digging into the floor. Fargo brought his forearm up, smashed it into the man's throat, and the figure fell away, gagging. The man reached for the knife to pull it out of the floor when Fargo brought a left around in a wild swing, crashing the blow into the side of his assailant's head. The figure fell backward, one hand flailing the air as he tried to reach the knife. Spinning, Fargo reached for the knife and had to twist away as the man sent a kick at him that caught him high on the shoulder. Fargo half turned, saw the man reaching for his gun, and flung himself forward in a half roll, half dive.

He slammed into the man as the gun lifted and a shot exploded, the bullet crashing into the wall. Fargo's hand closed around the man's gun hand, twisted hard, and heard the man curse in pain as his wrist bent backward. The gun fell from his fingers and Fargo brought his own fist down in a sideways blow that landed on the man's cheek, and brought another curse of pain. Fargo rose up, diving for the gun, but the intruder grabbed him around the chest and the gun went skittering across the floor. Fargo twisted and managed to shake off the man. He rolled and again went for the gun when it landed against the baseboard of the room. He had reached it when he turned to see the figure diving headfirst out of the window. Scooping up the gun, he ran to the window, fired a shot at the fleeing figure as it vaulted onto a horse and raced away. The shot sent splinters from the edge of the house as the rider turned the corner and disappeared.

Footsteps and shouts came from outside the door and Fargo opened to see Clora and two men with drawn guns. "He's gone," Fargo said. "Came in through the window. That's his knife," he added, gesturing to the blade still imbedded in the floor." One of the men stepped in and one pulled the knife from the floor as Clora turned the lamp up and peered at Fargo.

"You all right?" she asked, and he nodded. "We heard the shot and came to see."

"He wanted to do it quietly with the knife," Fargo said, handing her the gun.

"Anything personal?" the woman asked.

"Never saw him before," Fargo answered.

She crinkled her face. "We don't get much of that sort of thing here. Maybe somebody made a mistake," she said. "Or figured you as a stranger with money."

"Maybe." He shrugged.

"Sorry about it. Consider your bill paid," the woman said as she left with the two men. Fargo slid the bolt on the door and returned to the bed. He lay awake and wondered about the incident. Clora's suggestions hadn't satisfied him, yet he had nothing better to offer and the attack clung, disturbing in the way of an undefined ache. He closed his eyes finally and slept again, this time until the night came to an end.

3

Saddling the Ovaro at the stable, Fargo walked in the morning sun to Caroline's and found her waiting with the six outriders she had hired. "This is Burt Hobbs," she said, introducing a man of medium build with a pleasant-enough manner and a bristly mustache. Fargo took in the others and with a practiced glance could see that they were all average hands, veterans of many ordinary jobs over many ordinary years.

"Heard about you, Fargo," Hobbs said. "Glad to be riding with you."

"Thanks." Fargo nodded.

"Clora stopped by, told me about the incident," Caroline said to Fargo. "One of those random things. Thank God you weren't hurt." Fargo nodded and turned as the wagon drove to a halt, Ben Smith at the reins. Fargo's brow instantly furrowed as he took in the wagon. His eyes first lingered at the heavy tan canvas that had been stretched over the top bows and stake sides, then his gaze moved over the body, the wheels, and finally to the high driver's seat. Caroline instantly picked up the sharp appraisal he gave the wagon. "Something wrong?" she questioned.

Fargo's frown stayed. "Wrong? Don't know if that's the word exactly," he said and shot a glance at Ben

Smith. "You notice anything about the wagon, old-timer?" he queried.

"Just picked it up and hurried over here," Ben Smith said.

"Have a look at it," Fargo said, and Ben swung to the ground, stepping back to survey the wagon.

"Owensboro mountain wagon, outfitted with a canvas top, oversized brake," he said.

"Think about the wagon that was attacked," Fargo said and watched the older man's eyes begin to widen.

"By God," Ben murmured. "Damn close."

"Almost identical," Fargo said. "Both Owensboros, both with twenty-eight-inch-high sides, ten-and-a-half-by-three-and-a-half-foot bodies, wheels forty-four and fifty-two inches on both, oil-soaked woodwork, and standard factory colors of green bodies and red wheels. The only difference is this one has a toolbox up front which most people wouldn't notice."

"It has to be a coincidence," Caroline broke in.

"I don't put much store in coincidences," Fargo said.

"But they happen," Caroline said.

"They do," he admitted.

"This is one of them," Caroline said firmly and began to have her outriders load the wagon. Fargo stood back as the boxes of serum, neatly tied with rope, were loaded onto the wagon, followed by Caroline's personal bags, and finally food and other supplies. Caroline stayed inside the house a few moments more and when she came out she wore a dark blue skirt and a light blue shirt that curved atop the long line of her breasts yet managed to be both proper and attractive, with long sleeves and buttons up to the neck. The sun was already beginning to burn down, and he wondered how long she could stand the buttoned-up propriety. "Let's roll," Caroline said and climbed onto the seat beside Ben. Taking another glance back as he swung onto the Ovaro, Fargo saw that there were three extra horses tied behind the wagon, one a long-legged gray gelding.

Moving out in front of the wagon, Fargo led the way out of town and quickly turned north. He knew it would be impossible to pick up a trail until they were far from town, well up into the plateaus and low hills and perhaps not even then. But the doctor's letter had mentioned a few markers and Fargo was confident he knew the one with the rock formations and stone arches. Not having to scan the land to pick up a trail let them make good time, perhaps a blessing in disguise, he reflected. He rode ahead, turned up, and climbed onto high ground, whenever he had the chance letting his eyes move back from where they had come. Each time, he grimaced and wondered if he was being too suspicious. Yet the world had taught him it was almost impossible to be too suspicious and his eyes continued to sweep back as they rode on.

The day had gone into afternoon when he turned west onto a narrow plain edged by low hills well covered with cottonwoods. They were a mile or so into the narrow plain when he saw the wagon moving down toward them from a break in the trees, the high prow and long, curved side lines unmistakable, even if the Percherons weren't hooked up to the shafts. Holly held the reins, Randi Howell beside her. Harry Adamson and Ernie Alden rode alongside the heavy converted hay wagon, and Fargo saw they also had brought extra horses, the animals following along on long tethers. As the canvas pulled back, Fargo saw Herb Baxter inside with Terry Jones. "Surprise," Holly called out.

"I doubt it," Fargo said dryly and waited as Ben Smith rolled up to a halt.

"What are you doing here?" Caroline snapped.

"Same thing you are, honey," Holly said sweetly. "Going to find the Turner wagons."

"I told you we were traveling alone," Caroline said.

"We just happened to be going this way. It's a free country," Holly said. "Paths cross."

Caroline glared at her and shifted her glare to Fargo. "She's right. It's a free country. Paths cross." He shrugged.

"Let's see that they don't cross too often." Caroline sniffed. "Move on," she snapped at Ben and he sent the wagon forward. "Faster," Caroline hissed and he urged the team on. Fargo hung back a moment and Holly tossed a somewhat smug smile at him as he rode forward. He caught up to Caroline and pulled alongside her.

"Slow down. Don't take it out on your horses," he said, and Ben pulled back on the reins without waiting for Caroline to answer.

"She has her nerve," Caroline muttered.

"I'm thinking they'll be the least of our problems," Fargo said. "Stay on this plain. I'll be back." Putting the pinto into a trot, he rode into the low hills, along the edge of the cottonwoods and then into the forest to the higher ground. He paused on a ledge, his eyes scanning the terrain at the rear, his trailman's gaze taking in the turn of the leaves, the movement of the air, the swoop of birds, and the sudden flight of deer, eyes that read the special language that belonged to all the wild creatures.

Satisfied there was only quiet behind them, he moved down to the narrow plain as dusk spread over the land. Then he rode to where the wagon approached and guided it to a half circle in the cottonwoods. Burt Hobbs had his men tether their horses a dozen feet away on the low branches at the edge of the half circle. The man named Denny took on the cook's chores and produced a meal of bacon and beans over a small fire. Night fell and Fargo stood at the edge of the trees after he finished eating. The firelight flickered some hundred yards back. "Those are real determined ladies," Ben Smith said as he stepped from the trees.

"As determined and as anxious as Caroline," Fargo said.

"You said they weren't schoolteachers. Still think that?" Ben asked.

"More than ever," Fargo said and drew a speculative glance from Ben.

"Then why are they calling themselves that?" Ben asked.

"Good question," Fargo said.

"Guess you figure to get the answer," Ben said.

"Maybe," Fargo said. "Meanwhile, let's keep this between us for now."

"You've my word," Ben said. "Now I'll get me some sleep." He hurried off on his slightly bowed legs and Fargo took down his own bedroll. Caroline lay under a blanket a few feet away, her pale yellow hair almost white under the moon. He closed his eyes and slept. The night was quiet, and when morning came he awoke, washed with his canteen, and was dressed before the others stirred. Denny made coffee and Fargo downed a tin mug before climbing onto the Ovaro. Caroline wore the blouse still buttoned up, the sleeves down, he noted as he paused beside her.

"Go straight. I'll be back for you," he said.

She nodded, casting a glance back where the big hay wagon could be seen preparing to move forward. "What about them?" she asked.

"Forget about them," he said. "See to your own wagon." She was wearing a furrowed brow as he sent the Ovaro forward along the narrow plateau. He again turned into the low hills. The plateau stayed long and level for another mile or so and then grew less smooth, one half of it turning to climb over rutted and furrowed land that led sharply west. When he surveyed the uneven path he saw that it cut the time westward by curving sharply while the smooth plateau made a long, slow circle. The rough passage could save some six hours or more, he guessed, and he rode back through the hills. The mountain wagon was below him and he kept going until he came to the big hay wagon, where Randi Howell had switched places with Holly.

He steered the Ovaro downward and rode to the wagon. Randi pulled the big Percherons to a halt. "Thought you ought to know you'll be on your own soon," he said. "I'll be taking Caroline over a rough path your wagon won't make."

"Don't be too sure," Holly said.

He allowed an impatient grunt. "My guess is no," he said. "Keep on the plateau. It makes a long, slow curve but it'll take you west eventually. Maybe we'll meet up somewhere."

"Maybe sooner than you think," Holly said, and he saw the others looking on, their faces set.

"Good luck," he said, turning the pinto away.

"Thanks for telling us," Holly called after him as he rode on. He climbed back into the hills and retraced his steps until he moved downward again and waited as Caroline rolled up where the plateau divided. He gestured to the rough, furrowed passage.

"Harder but shorter," he said.

"We can do it," Caroline said, but Ben's nod was not as confident. Fargo led the way until the passage turned sharply.

"Stay on it," he said and once again sent the Ovaro into the hills. He rode slowly. He frowned at the unshod pony prints that became more plentiful and stopped to pick up an armband that had been dropped. "Wind river Shoshoni," he muttered aloud as he studied the geometric design. "Way out of their territory," he added as he dropped the armband and rode on. It was midafternoon when he halted atop a hill that afforded a long view back, and he slowly scanned the land. He started to move the pinto forward when he pulled back, his brows lowering and his gaze focusing on a distant rise in the plateau. He caught the sway of the branches first. They were moving in a line, as if blown by a long gust of wind.

But it was no wind, he saw; the branches moved too steadily, their movement was too concentrated. He shifted his gaze to the tops of the trees, carefully scanning the air until he finally spied the small, faint spiral of dust. Thinned out by the trees, yet following along the path of the moving branches, it was a silent banner to the Trailsman. Horsemen, he muttered inwardly, his mouth pulling tight. At least six, maybe more, he guessed. They would have made better time riding the open land of the plateau. But they chose to stay in the trees, and there was a meaning in that. They weren't just riding. They were staying out of sight. They were well able to pick up wagon wheel tracks from where they rode, he realized.

He watched awhile longer as thoughts sifted through his mind, none of them reassuring. Finally, he sent the pinto down to meet up with the wagon where it jounced along the hard passage. Ben did his best to avoid the worst of the rocks and ruts. Burt Hobbs and the other outriders were spread out, letting their horses pick their own way along the trail. Caroline had left her seat beside

Ben to walk alongside the wagon. "Less weight for the team to pull along this terrible ground," she said as Fargo came up. Her face glistened under the hot sun and her pale coloring had a faint pink flush to it. Her shirt had grown damp and clung to her, outlining the long line of her breasts. She saw him appreciate the sight and pulled at the blouse, only to have it instantly settle back onto her skin.

"Someone once told me that the price of modesty was immodesty," Fargo remarked. "Roll up your sleeves and undo those top buttons." She tossed him a glare as he rode on, his eyes moving across the difficulty of the road. The thoughts that had settled into his mind pushed at him. Any pursuers would be also slowed by the road. He was always grateful for favors, even small ones, he pondered. Peering into the distance, he estimated it would be dark when they reached the end of the passage. Holly and the others crossed his mind. If his suspicions were right, they were in no danger. The thought was a paradox, reassuring and disturbing at the same time. He grimaced and steered the Ovaro around a large rock, helping the horse negotiate the passage. As he neared the end of the rutted stretch he saw his guess had been right as the sun began to drop below the horizon line.

The passage ended in a long field of dropseed grass dotted with brilliant yellow buttercups. Fargo put the horse into a canter until he found a stand of red cedar. He surveyed the forest and waited beside the Ovaro until the wagon rolled up just as the sun disappeared and night hurried to spread itself over the land. "Put the wagon a dozen feet from the trees," he ordered as he saw that Caroline had sleeves rolled up, the top of the blouse opened. He gave her an approving nod, to which she refused to respond. Fargo allowed himself time to share a meal of corn cakes and dried buffalo and rose to his feet while the others were still gathered around the small fire. "I'll be back," he said, and Caroline's frown was instant.

"You're not going to look after them, I hope," she said.

"Feeling a little guilty?" he returned.

"Absolutely not," she snapped.

"I'm going to see if we'll be having company," Fargo said, and the others joined Caroline's frown.

"What do you mean?" she asked.

"I'm not sure but I'll tell you when I get back," he said, pulling himself onto the Ovaro and riding away before she could ask more questions. He knew he rode with only suspicions clinging to him, but the picture of two wagons rose in his mind and refused to let him hide in the word *coincidence*. The moon cast a pale light as he rode back along the harsh passage and he halted every few minutes to draw the night air into his nostrils. He guessed he'd ridden perhaps an hour when he felt his nose twitch. The scent of horses perspiring after having been ridden hard drifted to him, along with the unmistakable odor of damp saddle leather. He dismounted, let the Ovaro's reins drop to the ground. The horse would stay there, he knew.

Walking forward, he took small, silent steps, being careful not to dislodge loose stones that covered the passage. He heard the voices before he saw the dark shapes in the blackness, a few still sitting up, the others stretched out wherever they could find a spot in the rutted road. He flattened himself on the ground to crawl closer. "Everybody understand?" one dark shape asked.

"Yep," another answered. "Pick off anybody we can see and pour so much lead into the wagon a mouse couldn't escape."

"Right. Nobody gets away this time. We hit them at dawn while they're just waking up," the first voice said. "Now everybody get some shut-eye." Fargo stayed, peered through the darkness, and counted eight shapes. As the sounds of sleep came to him he pushed himself backward until he rose and moved silently back to the Ovaro. He led the horse away for another twenty yards before climbing into the saddle. When he reached the wagon, Caroline and Ben Smith were standing by the empty shafts and Burt Hobbs and the other outriders came to gather around.

"We'll be having company come dawn," Fargo said.

"You mean, we're going to be attacked? We've been followed?" Caroline frowned.

"Bull's-eye," Fargo said.

"I don't understand this. Why? What's it all mean?" Caroline asked.

"I don't know but I'm sure of one thing. When they hit that other wagon, they thought they were hitting you," Fargo said. "A case of mistaken wagons."

Caroline peered hard at him. "Then that attack on you wasn't . . ."

"A random thing?" Fargo cut in. "That's right. Word was out I'd be breaking trail for you. Somebody figured that without me you'd never find the Turner wagons."

"But why? It makes no sense," Caroline said.

"Maybe I can pull a little of it together," Fargo said. "But tomorrow. Right now we've got to get ready and get in a little sleep." He turned to Burt Hobbs. "Your boys would bed down somewhere near the wagon, right?" he asked and Hobbs nodded. "I want you to put out your bedrolls or blankets same as you'd normally do. Only tonight you'll bunch extra clothes so's it'll look like you're asleep inside them." The others nodded and he turned back to Caroline. "You hang your outfit outside the wagon as though you're airing it out. It'll make them sure you're still in the wagon."

"Where will I be?" she asked.

"In the trees with the rest of us," Fargo said. "We'll be in a semicircle lying a few feet from each other. They'll come pouring lead into the bedrolls and the wagon to kill us while we're still asleep. But we'll do the surprising. Now let's start laying everything out."

He took his own bedroll down, put it near the rear of the wagon, bunched extra clothes in it to give it shape, and when he finished, Caroline had hung her blouse and skirt on a hanger on the tailgate of the wagon. She faced him wearing a light blue robe that clung to the slenderness of her. He surveyed the scene when everyone was finished and satisfied that everything appeared normal, he led the way into the trees. "Rifles, everybody," he said.

"I don't have a rifle," Caroline said.

"I've got an extra one," Ben Smith said and stepped away for a moment to return with a heavy old Hawkens.

"I'll start here," Fargo said, lying down just inside the edge of the cedar. "You next to me," he ordered Caroline, pointing to a spot a few feet from him. She settled down with the rifle, Ben Smith taking a place a few feet from her, and the others lying down until they had formed the semicircle that looked out at the wagon and the bedrolls and blankets. "There's plenty of time to get some sleep," Fargo said.

"Suppose we don't wake up soon enough?" Caroline asked.

"I'll wake up in time," Fargo said. "I'll wake you. You pull on Ben and wake him and so on down the line. Nobody fires until I do, then shoot as fast and as straight as you can. He heard the others stretch and settle themselves and he looked at Caroline. She stared out at the wagon, her eyes wide, her face tense. He reached out, closed one hand around her arm and kept it there. She looked at him and he felt her slowly relax, her pale, delicate coloring almost ghostlike in the dimness of the moonlight. She let out a long, slow sigh, finally.

"Thank you," she whispered. "I'll be all right, now." He drew his hand from around her arm. She closed her eyes and put her head down and it wasn't too long when he heard the steady, faint sound of her breathing as she slept. He put the big Henry in the crook of his arm as he set his mental alarm clock and pulled sleep around himself. The very first touch of pink edged the horizon as Fargo snapped up, blinked sleep away, and reached out to put his hand over Caroline's face. She lay on her side, her eyes coming open instantly with a moment of fright, then her body relaxing as she saw him. "Wake Ben," he said and watched her turn and reach out and pull at the figure beside her.

"Wake Burt," he heard her whisper before turning back to him. The faint pink line moved quickly and became a soft pink glow as the new day proclaimed itself. He put his forehead down against the earth, his wild-creature hearing tuned to the soft, soughing sounds of the wind, the earth, the touch of claw or pad. But it was the vibration that came to him first, the ground responding to the assault of hooves. He listened for a moment longer and raised his head. His eyes were focused on the cedars almost directly across from where he lay.

"Get ready," he said, bringing the rifle to his shoulder.

"Get ready," Caroline whispered to Ben, and the words were passed down the line. The new dawn held the morning in its gray-pink light as the riders burst into sight at a full gallop, racing along the ground to the wagon and the bedrolls. Fargo waited for the attackers to start pouring bullets into the wagon before his finger tightened on the trigger of the big Henry. His shot sent one of the attackers flying from his horse and instantly the woods erupted in a deadly hail of gunfire. Fargo saw three more of the attackers topple from their horses, then two more. The last two, wheeling in surprise and confusion, tried to race across the field but were cut down by another cascade of gunfire from inside the trees.

Fargo pushed to his feet and walked from the trees. The others followed him as he knelt beside one of the still figures. "See if they've anything on them," he said as he began to go through the man's pockets.

"Nothing," Burt Hobbs called out after a few moments. "Just the usual cowhand's junk. Nothing to tell you anything."

"Didn't expect there would be," Fargo said.

"You said you could pull some of this together," Ben reminded him.

"Not here," Caroline said quickly, turning away from the figures that littered the ground. "We going to bury them?" she asked, still looking away.

"They don't deserve burying. They were going to kill us while we were asleep," Burt Hobbs said.

"It'll take some hours. You said time was everything," Fargo put in. "Your call, Caroline."

"Let's go on, quickly," she said, starting for the wagon. "What'll happen to their horses?"

"They'll find their way someplace," Fargo said, and she took her things from the hanger and hurried into the wagon. Ben hitched up the team as everyone gathered their things. The sun was hot and bright when Fargo led the way across the field of buttercups, too many flecked with red. He rode at a good pace, leaving the grim scene behind and finally pulling up at a small pond. As canteens were refilled and the horses drank, Caroline swung from the wagon to face him, her eyes still troubled.

"It was so brutal," she said with a shiver.

"You could've been on the other end," Fargo said evenly and she nodded but the pain stayed in her pale blue orbs. "Let's talk now," Caroline said, and Ben Smith stepped closer.

"They were hired by someone in the Turner wagons before they left Green Springs," Fargo said. "Somebody in the Turner wagons wanted to make sure nobody followed them. Of course, whoever did it didn't know anything about a possible smallpox outbreak. He was strictly following his own agenda. When you talked it all over town that you were going after the Turner wagons, his hired hands just waited for the moment to get you."

"Only they hit that other wagon by mistake," Ben said.

"When they found that out they sat back for another chance," Fargo said. "This much seems pretty clear now."

"But who's afraid of being followed? And why?" Caroline asked.

"Could be anybody. Who knows?" Ben answered.

"Does it make any difference?" Caroline thought aloud. "We know it's not us they're afraid of."

"It might make a damn big difference," Fargo said. "Somebody on that train is very afraid, afraid enough to hire a passel of killers. They want to make sure nobody catches up to them. We do that and they might do damn near anything. I don't want to take a bullet because somebody thinks I could have been sent after them."

"Well, I'm certainly not going to stop going after the train," Caroline said.

"Didn't say you should but I'd like to get a lead on who our boy might be. You've a list of who's on that wagon train?" Fargo asked.

"Yes, Doc Dodson left it with me," she said. She stepped into the wagon and returned with a sheet of paper. "Frank and Inez Turner," she began. "They organized the train. They're from Kansas, where he was a farmer. Bad crops did them in and they're looking for a fresh start. They have one wagon, it says here."

"That seems harmless enough," Fargo said.

"Tom and Sarah Barnett," Caroline read. "They have a boy and a girl and she's pregnant. They're from Nebraska. He ran a store and didn't do well at it, dry goods. They wanted to try someplace else. Two wagons, one filled with merchandise. Next are Ed and Beth Osgood from South Dakota. They have two young boys. He's a cooper looking for a new place to practice his trade. Two wagons, one filled with his tools."

"What happened to his trade where he was?" Fargo questioned.

"Doesn't say here," Caroline answered. "The third family is the Torrances, Carl and Eva and Eva's parents. Eva's the other pregnant one on the train. They're all the way from Iowa where they had a herd that died on them. The next is Lila Tomkins."

"The schoolteacher, the one Holly Crater and the other two women want to reach," Fargo said.

"That's right. She's traveling alone in her own wagon."

"It say where she taught school?" Fargo asked.

Caroline peered at the paper. "No," she said. "Next is Donald Burton. He's driving a one-horse spring wagon."

"Bad for hard roads, good for fast travel," Fargo commented.

"He's a banker from Oklahoma. He joined the Turner wagons to scout out territories for new banks. Next is Orrin Dodge, from Kansas. He's a lumberman out to find new opportunities."

"Kansas isn't lumberman's country," Fargo murmured.

"No wagon," Caroline read. "On horseback with a pack mule. The last two are Aaron Stillman and Bettie Stillman. They're traveling artists with one wagon." She halted and folded the slip of paper. "I don't see any villains in that bunch," she said.

"Villains don't wear signs," Fargo grunted.

"I still don't see what you can learn from this," she said.

"Nothing right out front but maybe I'll come across something after I think some more," he said. "Let's move." Swinging onto the pinto, he led the way along the soft field. His eyes searched for the place where he expected the other, longer road would curve to meet the field when he saw the unexpected opening appear in the trees. His brows lifted further as the converted hay-wagon rolled into sight. "I'll be damned. Didn't expect you'd be along this soon," he said to Holly.

"Never underestimate what Percherons can do. We decided to follow you on the hard road but it was no good and we went back to the other. Halfway along we saw this cut, just wide enough for the wagon. We took it and here we are," Holly said. "Thought you'd be further on."

"Unexpected delay," Fargo said, and Caroline offered nothing more.

"Keep moving," she ordered Ben, who sent the wagon on.

"See you," Holly said to Fargo with a bright smile which he returned as he rode away and saw the hay wagon wheel around to follow.

"I suppose they'll be dogging us again until we put some distance between us," Caroline muttered as Fargo came alongside the wagon.

"Probably," he said and rode on, leaving them behind knowing they'd follow his tracks. As he rode, he felt the ground softening under the Ovaro's steps and his glance took in long beds of cardinal flowers, their robes of brilliant red blossoms standing sharply against their deep green leaves. Deep yellow clusters of marsh marigolds also began to appear. Both flowers gave signs of woods and fields that were moistened by water that seeped through the ground not all that far away. No small pond, nothing quiet and contained, he deduced, a body of water that ran freely with strength enough to permeate the land. Any doubts in his mind were dispelled when he saw the mottled-red cabbagey leaves of a line of skunk cabbage.

He halted the horse, aware that water could mean many things, not all of them good. He scanned the cedars at his right and spotted a break in the trees. Then he nosed the horse forward into what turned out to be a leafy, narrow tunnel that ran deep into the woods. He followed it to the end, where it formed a thick-leafed cul-de-sac, well hidden away. Turning, he rode to the field as the afternoon sun began to move across the sky. He waved to Caroline for the wagon to follow him and then led the way into the green tunnel, halting where it ended. "Wait here till I get back. Rest the horses and relax," he said.

"What is it?" Caroline frowned as Burt Hobbs and his men dismounted.

"Going to check out what's ahead. Meanwhile, I don't want you out in the open. Been seeing too many Indian signs," he said, pausing for a moment. "I'm going to send Holly's wagon in here, too," he told her.

"You've no need to see to them," Caroline said. "They're on their own."

"I'm not seeing to them," he said.

"What do you call it?" She frowned.

"Seeing to my conscience," he said and rode back through the narrow opening, returned to the open field, and waited till Holly and the others rolled up. "Go down that opening and stay there," he told her.

"You say it, I do it." Holly smiled. "Expecting trouble?"

"Don't know but I like to find trouble before it finds me," Fargo said. As soon as the heavy wagon was out of sight in the trees, he rode on, traveling slowly and as the skunk cabbage grew more thickly alongside the field he decided to dismount. The Ovaro following behind, he walked forward and felt the ground grow still softer under his steps. He pulled the horse into the trees, dropped the reins over a low branch, and went on alone. The field narrowed and he'd only gone a few hundred yards more when he smelled the smoke and the odor of camass root and prairie turnip. He edged forward along the trees until the scene opened before him. His eyes went to the river, first. It was wide and moving with majestic slowness, the source of the water that seeped through the ground as it probably had for hundreds of years.

Slowly, his eyes moved across the camp that stretched along the riverbank. No hunting camp, he saw at once, but a full and complete base camp with squaws and kids, old men and young braves. The earth pits stretched along the west end of the camp, where the food was being boiled and tended by four squaws. Southern Arapaho, Fargo figured as he studied the markings on the teepees and armbands worn by some of the braves. He counted eight of the broad-based teepees favored by the Arapaho, with another three set at the edge of the river instead of spread throughout the camp. Horses were tied on a long rope at the far end of the camp.

His eyes scanned the camp again and he saw two bare-breasted squaws tending a dozen fish on a salmon-drying rack near the water. Four pyramids of dry vegetable husks and rinds were spread through the camp, saved for use in cooking fires. A quick count told him the camp held at least thirty braves. He surveyed the entire camp again and noted there were little piles of blankets folded outside many of the teepees. He grimaced at what that told him. He took in the river again and followed the direction of the wind where it blew against the sandbar willows at the water's edge. His face was drawn tight as he began to back away to the trees as the sun dipped to the distant horizon. He returned to the Ovaro and walked the horse back, climbing into the saddle after another fifty yards, and finally rode into the narrow leafy tunnel.

He was unhappy. Caroline would be even more unhappy at what he'd tell her, he realized. But he was just the messenger. The Arapaho were sending the message.

4

"You can't be serious," Caroline said, staring incredulously at him. "Go all the way back and find some other way?"

"I'm real serious. You can't cross the river anywhere near here. The wind blows downriver. You cross upriver and they'll smell you. You cross downriver and they'll hear you," Fargo said.

"You can't be sure of that. They'll be asleep," Caroline said.

"Many of the braves sleep outside the teepees. If even one wakes, and I promise you at least one will wake, you're finished. He'll hear you, smell you, or sense you," Fargo answered.

"Finding another route or going all the way downriver will cost us at least a day," she said.

"Maybe two," he agreed.

"That's out of the question. We can't lose that much time. We cross near here someplace," she insisted.

"Suicide. Look, you can't deliver the serum if you're dead. You won't do them any good that way," Fargo said.

"I won't do them any good if we're too late," Caroline returned adamantly and he swore silently at her answer. It summed up the core of the dilemma. "God knows what other delays we might still meet," she added and he couldn't deny that, either.

With his mouth a thin line, he swept a glance at the others, who he knew looked to him for a solution. He swore under his breath. "We move out of here," he said and sent the Ovaro along the tree-lined tunnel, no decisions made, only the recognition that they had to retreat. The night descended as he led the way back over the field, Caroline behind him, the hay wagon following. He rode as the moon began to rise in the night sky, finally reaching a place where the cedars grew sparse, offering another pathway to the river. He took the offering as his mind raced with thoughts and plans he examined, discarded, and replaced. When he smelled the river he drew to a halt while they were still in the trees, dismounted and turned to Caroline as the others looked on. "There might be a way you can cross the river here and stay alive," he said.

"How?" he heard Ben Smith ask before Caroline could.

"If the Arapaho are too busy to hear, smell, or sense you're crossing," Fargo said.

"How the hell is that going to happen?" Ben grunted.

"By creating a diversion that'll keep them from paying attention to anything but their own problems," Fargo said.

"How do you figure to do that?" Ben asked.

"By setting their whole camp on fire," Fargo said. The mixture of emotions running through the faces staring at him ranged from surprise, to disbelief, to uncertainty, to hope. "There'll be one chance and everything has to go right," he said. "It's going to take all of you."

"I'll cross with the wagon. You can use Ben, Burt, and the rest of the men," Caroline said.

"No. Ben drives. Burt and his boys go along. I don't know how deep or how fast that river runs. Everything will be for nothing if you get stuck. I want riders with you if you've trouble. I'll use Holly and her crew," Fargo said.

"Whatever you want," Holly put in.

"I'll want you, Randi, and Ernie Alden," Fargo said. "He's the youngest of us. He can run fast." Ernie Alden shrugged and his owlish face seemed faintly pleased. Fargo took Caroline aside, his voice lowered so only she could hear. "They help us, they'll deserve to go along with us afterwards. That'd be only fair," he said.

"I guess so," Caroline agreed with only a tinge of reluctance and he returned to the others.

"Terry can drive your wagon across. Adamson and Baxter will ride with you. Burt can help if you're in trouble," he said and the young woman nodded gravely. "Move to the edge of the river and wait there. You'll be able to see the glow of the flames. When you do, take both wagons across the river and keep going after you reach the other side. We'll catch up to you. I hope," he added grimly. He stepped back and watched as the wagons began to move away. When they were out of sight he turned to the two girls and Ernie Alden, who was plainly the most nervous of the three. "Take off your clothes," he said, starting to pull his shirt off.

"Why?" Randi frowned.

"We'll be crawling to the edge of the camp. We can't have any fabric that rustles, any clothes that smell of perfume, wool, leather. The Indian has a nose like a damn raccoon. Strip down to your drawers," he said as he continued to undress until he had on only his gunbelt and his drawers. Holly and Randi undressed to half slips and he saw that Randi had a lovely torso, breasts smaller than Holly but higher and firmer. "Wish I had more time," he murmured and drew smiles from both. Ernie Alden kept sneaking embarrassed glances at them, Fargo noted. "Stay with me," he said as he started off at a long lope, halting when he reached the Indian camp. He saw the sleeping figures on the blankets that dotted the camp and listened for the sound of voices from inside the teepees. There were none and satisfied that the camp was held in the grip of deep, new sleep, he moved forward again before dropping to one knee. He handed each of the young women six long lucifers from the waistband of his drawers. "You know how to light these?" he asked.

"Strike them against each other," Holly said.

"Go to the far end of the camp and set fire to the edges of all the teepees at that end. Soon as they're burning, you come back here," Fargo said. "Go." Staying on one knee, he watched as Holly and Randi carefully moved along the edge of the camp to the very end, where they were swallowed up by the night. Moving forward on careful steps, he beckoned to Ernie Alden and handed the man four more of the lucifers and pointed to two of the four pyramids of dry husks and rinds. "You set fire to those two," he said. "Soon as you see the teepees start to burn. Light them and run."

"You expect they'll burn fast?" Ernie Alden asked.

"They're so dry and tightly packed they'll all but explode," Fargo said. "Now, get over to them." The man moved away and Fargo drew two more of the long matchsticks and crept toward the first of the two pyramids near him. He crouched down behind the nearest, peered along the camp to the far end, and waited. It seemed an interminable time but he knew it was only seconds and he cursed under his breath as he saw a blanketed figure turn, sit up for a moment, and then lie back down again. The sudden leap of orange caught his eye, grew stronger, and traveled along the line of teepees. It was time. Fargo struck the two matches together and both flared up at once. He tossed one into the pyramid, ducked and running in a crouch, crossed to the second pyramid and threw the match into it.

He was racing away when he half turned to see both pyramids erupt, instantly creating their own outward draft. Husks and rinds skyrocketed upward and outward, borne by the self-created explosive drafts, each a fiery missile that sailed through the air to land against the teepees that dotted the camp. He saw the two pyramids Elden had set afire exploding, the husks and rinds arching through the air. Not unlike huge Arapaho fire arrows, he reflected. In seconds, almost every teepee was on fire, their dry hides quick to burn. But braves were on their feet and figures raced from inside the teepees, some fighting flames that engulfed them.

Fargo reached the ground beyond the edge of the camp, dove, and rolled, regaining his balance to rest on one knee. Ernie Alden was running in a crouch to him. He peered past the man and saw Holly and Randi crawling their way toward him. Inside the Indian camp, bedlam had broken out as teepees went up in flames and burning husks and rinds continued to shoot into the air. He saw figures racing back and forth to the river's edge, braves, squaws, and children, each desperately finding something to carry water, leaky baskets, moccasins, shirts, hollowed-out gourds, blankets held by the edges to hold water, and pieces of hollow logs. As he watched, he saw four braves pull a canoe half filled with water to the center of the camp, where others used their hands and cooking utensils to fling water up at the burning teepees.

They would be at their tasks for at least another hour, an exercise in futility, he knew. Everything burned too fast and too furiously. By midnight they would be wetting down only charred bits and pieces of the camp. He gestured to Holly and staying in a crouch began to run. If there had been no problems, the wagons were across the river by now. The diversion had worked, a good omen, perhaps, he hoped. They reached where they had left the horses, pulled on clothes, and Holly rode the Ovaro with him while Randi rode with Ernie Alden. The river was silent and empty when they reached it and Fargo allowed himself a final sigh of relief. He eased the Ovaro into the water and led the way across, picked up the wagon tracks on the other side, and halted to smooth them out for some hundred yards or so. When they largely vanished of themselves where the thick dropseed grass sprung up, he went on and caught up with the wagons.

"Done," he said. "We got away with it."

"You pulled it off, Fargo," Ben said admiringly.

"We ride till midnight, put some more distance between us," Fargo said and sent the Ovaro forward, exploring a narrow passage between twin stands of red cedar. When the midnight moon reached the high sky, he found a leafy alcove and waved the wagons into it. As everyone prepared to sleep, he wandered to where Holly stood beside the hay wagon, a short nightshirt resting lightly on her solid body. "You'll be coming along with us from now on," he said.

She gave him a slow, appreciative smile and brought her lips to his. "Whenever you want," she murmured.

"I'll remember that," he said as he strolled away. He

had gone off by himself, his bedroll laid out, when Caroline came by.

"You tell her they'll be going with us?" she asked.

"I did. She thanked me," Fargo said.

"I'm sure she'll do better," Caroline said with a note of disdain.

"Pull your claws in. She's a schoolteacher," Fargo said.

She raised one eyebrow. "I wonder about that," she said. Fargo sorted words in his mind.

"Why?" he asked.

"Woman's intuition." She shrugged and walked away. He stared after her, surprised and not surprised. He'd had more than enough experience with woman's intuition to very thoroughly respect it. He wouldn't tell her he also wondered. He wouldn't be able to come up with so simple a reason. He shed clothes, lay down and welcomed sleep until the new day came. As the others readied the wagons, he shared coffee and bacon with Ben Smith.

"You worked it in real smooth," Ben said to him.

"Worked what in?" Fargo frowned.

"Getting Caroline to have Holly and the others come along," the older man said.

"Thought it was the fair thing to do," Fargo said blandly.

"That wasn't your only reason." Ben chuckled.

Fargo gave him a penetrating, sidelong glance. "How'd you get to be such an old fox?" he asked.

"Comes with old age," Ben said.

"Hell it does," Fargo returned.

Ben laughed. "All right, comes with being a natural-born skeptic."

"I'll go with that," Fargo said.

"You still haven't answered me," Ben said.

"Got to thinking how things always find a way to fit," Fargo said. "When somebody's running it's usually damn certain somebody's chasing. We know somebody in the Turner wagons is running. Somebody there is real afraid of being caught. Now, we can't figure who that might be from here but maybe we can figure out who's doing the chasing."

Ben's lips pursed in thought. "Those dry-gulchers had orders to stop anyone following the Turner wagons. They heard about Caroline and went after her. But we know she's not chasing anybody," he said.

"And we know we've a wagonload of folks real anxious to get to the Turner train," Fargo said.

"You think three of them are lying about being schoolteachers," the older man said.

"That's right but maybe they're not the only ones playing games," Fargo said. "Little things don't fit right."

"Such as?"

"Ernie Alden says he's a traveling salesman. I've seen a couple hundred traveling salesmen. They're all of a type, loud, smooth talkers, always there with a story or a joke, brassy and pushy. Alden's so quiet he's almost mousy. He's not like any traveling salesman I've ever met."

"He sure isn't," Ben agreed. "And the others?"

"Don't have a line on them yet but I wonder about Herb Baxter. Have you watched him at all?"

"Yes. Keeps to himself, hardly talks to anyone. Never saw a man with such a tight mouth," Ben said.

"He says he's very concerned over his friends on the Turner train, Aran and Bettie Stillman, but he looks like a man who's brooding and angry, not concerned," Fargo said. "Of course, I'm doing a lot of supposing, I'll admit."

Ben Smith's eyes crinkled. "About schoolteachers, too?" he queried.

"No, no supposing there." Fargo laughed. "I'll be finding out why in time. Now, let's get rolling." He climbed onto the pinto and the two wagons followed as he led the way along a trail that rose into high plains country. He let memory guide him and by midday he rode alongside the long forest of gambel oak Dodson had mentioned in his letter. He rode to the end of the forest, waved the wagons into a sharp right, and moved along a flat field until he halted again where the inverted scarlet petals of the wild columbine formed a brilliant carpet as far as the eye could see. The second marker the doctor had referred to in his letter and now Fargo turned sharply right when the columbine finally came to an end.

The route climbed upward, but not too steeply for the wagons and the day was drawing to a close when he came to the tall rock formations, the natural arches, and stone windows forming a cathedral-like series of arches and Gothic curves. "We bed down here. Tomorrow we go north. There's a way station. I'm sure they stopped there. Maybe I can pick up a trail from there," he said.

"Have you stopped at the way station?" Caroline asked.

"Yes. It has good wells and enough rooms for a stage full of travelers," Fargo said. "It's pretty isolated but the stage drivers know of it. It's run by a shifty, shady character named Mexico Jack. Seems he lived in Mexico until he had to leave."

"Good night," Caroline said, and he saw the strain of the hard day in her face, her delicate coloring even paler than usual. He had set a hard pace and he felt the pull on his own body as he set out his bedroll. Denny didn't make the effort to find firewood and served up strips of cold beef jerky. Fargo stretched and watched Harry Adamson nervously smoke three cigarettes before he went to sleep. The night stayed quiet, save for the distant howls of timber wolves, and when morning came the sun quickly grew hot. While Fargo dressed, he noticed that Adamson was rationing the water from his canteen.

"We'll have fresh water by noon," he called to the man and Adamson nodded gratefully.

"Haven't got the hang of saving water yet," the man said. "Never had to do it."

"You a banker, too, like your friend with the Turner wagons?" Fargo inquired casually.

"No, no, I worked in a store, as a carpenter," Adamson said quickly.

"Good, honest work," Fargo said and grunted inwardly. Adamson not only never had to save water, he had hands that never used a hammer or a saw, hands that were smooth and soft without the hint of a nick, bruise, or scar. He found himself wondering if anyone with Holly was what they claimed to be and he took a moment to watch her climb onto the wagon. She continued to exude an open-faced cheerfulness and that part of her was no mask and made him wonder about the other part of her even more. He turned to saddling the Ovaro and when he finished he saw Caroline beside Ben on her wagon. She had changed to a short-sleeved, loose white blouse, a thin material that rested lightly on the long curve of her breasts. The sun gave her pale coloration a faint flush that made her seem as though she were porcelain. But there was steel underneath, he had come to know.

He led the wagons north where the land grew dry and

juniper began to predominate. Again, he set a hard pace and the Percherons fell back, but were fresher than Caroline's team when he halted for a break. It was noon when the way station came into view, a collection of flat buildings against the flat land. The first thing he saw was some seven men lounging against a splintered corral where four cows lay in the sun and half a dozen hogs gathered around a feed trough. He remembered the main building of the inn as he approached, though it had been some years since he'd seen it, flat-roofed, sprawling with three wings, a stable at the rear, bunkhouses alongside the stable. Two large wells were behind the main building and Fargo saw a slender figure emerge from the front door of the inn as he rode to a halt, a slip of a girl in a one-piece dress that for all its shapeless raggedness she somehow wore with insouciance.

She let dark brown, almost black eyes move up and down him as he dismounted, taking in the two wagons and the people with them. Olive-skinned, black hair falling below her shoulders and in need of a combing, she had an unkempt sultriness to her. "You come for rooms?" she asked.

"No, for some answers. Mexico Jack here?" Fargo asked.

"I'll get him. I am Melita," she said.

"How long have you been here, Melita?" Fargo inquired.

"Mexico Jack bring me here two years ago," she said and the dark brown eyes held his face appraisingly before she slowly turned and sauntered back to the building, letting her hips sway as she went.

"Bold one," Caroline said disapprovingly.

"She doesn't hide what she's thinking. That's not always bold. Sometimes it's just honest," Fargo said and he let his eyes move past Caroline to Holly. She returned a nod that was as much careful as it was agreement. Melita returned a few moments later, walking a few paces behind Mexico Jack as he came outside. The man's eyes took in the two wagons with a fast glance and then focused in on Fargo, a slight frown digging into his brow.

"It has been a while since you passed this way, big man," Mexico Jack said, and Fargo nodded, taking in the tall, lithe body of the man, the pencil-thin mustache, and the long sideburns that were part of a face that was handsome in the way a coral snake is handsome. Mexico Jack wore the same black sombrero that rested against his back as the last time he'd been there, Fargo noted, along with the short, black vest with silver embroidery. Mexico Jack studied Fargo, his eyes narrowed. "You are the one who they call the Trailsman. It comes back to me," Mexico Jack said.

"You've a good memory," Fargo said.

"Fargo," the man said, snapping his fingers, plainly pleased with himself. Fargo returned a nod and Mexico Jack took in the others with a smoothly charming smile. "Welcome to my inn. You will want rooms and a good meal. We do our humble best," he said.

"No rooms," Fargo said. "We want to know about a wagon train that passed this way."

"Many wagon trains come this way," the man said, almost chidingly.

"Not that many," Fargo corrected. "A man named Turner led this one. Nine wagons."

"There was a doctor with them," Caroline cut in. "It's very important we find them. They may be in a lot of trouble if we don't." Fargo shot her a hard glance, which she ignored.

"Trouble?" Mexico Jack echoed.

"There may be an epidemic on the train, smallpox. We're carrying the serum they may have to have. It's the only thing that can save them," Caroline said.

Mexico Jack's lips pursed in thought, his eyes staying on Caroline. "*Caramba*. This serum, it is very valuable," he said.

"Very. To anybody. But their lives depend on it. So you see, it's terribly important if you can remember," Caroline said.

"The lady exaggerates a little," Fargo said.

"I'm not exaggerating at all," Caroline said reproachfully. "They must have that serum."

Mexico Jack frowned in thought for a moment, then threw his hands upward. "I'm sorry, my friends. They did not pass this way," he said.

"I know they came by the stone arches. This would be their next logical stop. I can't see their going any other way," Fargo said.

Mexico Jack's eyes went to Caroline and he shrugged sympathetically. "But they did," he said.

"Yes, that's obvious," Caroline said.

"It doesn't make any damn sense," Fargo said and his eyes moved past Mexico Jack, pausing at Melita, and staying there. She looked and listened with eyes slightly narrowed, a single furrow causing a tiny frown across her forehead, though she kept the rest of her face expressionless. She felt his eyes on her, glanced at him, and quickly looked away. He watched her a moment longer but she refused to glance at him again.

Holly's voice cut into his musings. "Shouldn't we be moving on?"

"Yes," he said, frowning as he wheeled the Ovaro in a tight circle. "Let's go." He shot another glance at Melita

71

and saw her turn away. His stomach tight, he waved the others forward and set out, riding with dark uneasiness pulling at him. He rode north, across the dry land and alongside a line of alligator junipers when he heard the horse coming up behind him and turned to see Burt Hobbs.

"Caroline wants to see you," the man said, and Fargo turned to follow the man back to the wagon. Caroline had Ben pull to a halt.

"Why are we going this way?" Caroline asked. "We should go back and find another trail. They didn't come this way."

"So I heard," Fargo said with a grunt.

She frowned at him. "Are you saying they did come this way? That they stopped at the way station?"

"I'm saying I'll bet my ass this is the way they came. Maybe they came by at night and nobody saw them," Fargo said.

She frowned in thought. "I suppose that would be possible," she murmured.

"And another thing. From now on, don't talk so much," Fargo said gruffly.

"I was only explaining why it's so important we reach the Turner wagons. What harm could that do?" Caroline said.

"I don't know but from now on I'll do the talking," he said.

"I object to your attitude." Caroline bristled.

"Fine. Object all you want but do it in silence," Fargo said and sent the Ovaro forward, aware that the turmoil inside him was not just due to Caroline. Something was wrong. The Turner wagons would have passed the way station, he told himself again. Trailing was not just finding tracks. Trailing was knowing the ways of man and beast. Trailing was an inner sense you developed as surely as a plant develops flowers. And sometimes it was a girl whose face spoke when her lips didn't. Spotting a break in the junipers, he waited and waved the others into the leafy alcove. "You'll camp here," he said.

"We've two hours of day left," Caroline protested.

"Then you can all get some extra rest," Fargo said from the saddle.

She peered at him. "You're going back to the way station, aren't you?" she asked. "Why?"

"Maybe there's something I missed," he said and returned a skeptical glance.

"I think you just can't stand having made a mistake," she said.

"Close," he snapped and sent the Ovaro into a fast canter, holding it all the way back to the way station, where he rode to a halt and slid from the saddle. He took in the half-dozen figures lounging near the bunkhouse and saw them move away as he walked to the main house. They wandered to the corrals, he noted, busying themselves in a desultory fashion. The slender figure of Melita came from the inn, still in the one-piece dress, but she had run a comb through her black hair. She looked less unkempt but no less sultry, her almost-black eyes regarding him with a challenge in their boldness. She uttered a tiny snort when she saw him.

"I expected you'd come back," she said.

"Why?" he asked.

She allowed the edge of a smile and he saw that her features were both even and strong, an olive-skinned beauty to her behind the smudged and waiflike outer appearance. "You're not the kind that is fooled," she said.

"What are you saying?" he asked.

She shrugged. "Just that," she said.

"Bullshit, honey," he said. "Where's Mexico Jack?"

"Gone away," she said, leaning against the edge of the door. Fargo saw small points press into the one-piece garment as she held her torso forward.

"How old are you, Melita?" he asked.

"Fifteen," she said.

"You said Mexico Jack brought you here two years ago?"

"Yes," she said. Mexico Jack liked them young, Fargo noted silently.

"When will he be back?" he asked.

"I don't know." Melita shrugged.

"Where'd he go?" Fargo questioned and she shrugged.

"I don't know," she said.

"I think you do," Fargo said.

She gave another shrug. "I can try to remember," she said.

"You try. Meanwhile, I'll look around," he said and she stayed at the door, not moving. He sauntered away, his eyes sweeping the yard and the bunkhouse, narrowing as he scanned the building. It had been scrubbed down, he saw, the wood still showing the broom and brush marks, and he stepped closer, halting as the still-sharp odor of strong soap came to him. He drew in a deep breath and smelled lye with creosote added for extra strength. Slowly, he walked around the bunkhouse and saw that the entire structure had been scrubbed down with the extra-strong soap. Buildings were sometimes washed down, he pondered, but with an ordinary soap, and a new coat of paint was the most common method of sprucing up a structure. The frown digging into his forehead, he walked on past the bunkhouse and came upon two small tombstones near a hog pen. He went to the spot, stared down at the two graves, both with freshly dug soil. He finally turned away as Melita approached, a feline beauty in the way her slender body moved.

"Sudden accidents?" he said, nodding to the two graves.

Her face set, she answered without looking at him. "Sort of," she murmured.

"Talk, Melita," Fargo growled, his voice changing character. "I'm getting bothered by you."

"Two of the hands came down suddenly, shaking, high fever, their whole bodies breaking out with sores and they die, just like that they die. Mexico Jack had the whole bunkhouse washed down," she said.

"After the wagon train passed this way, wasn't it?" Fargo said, and she nodded, her face sober. "Did the wagons stop overnight? Did people stay in the rooms?" Fargo questioned.

"No. They stopped overnight but nobody stayed in the rooms," Melita said. "They stayed in their wagons and bought water and supplies. The two hands that died brought most of the water barrels to them."

Fargo's lips grew tight as he listened to the girl. Two questions had been answered. He had been right about one. The wagons had passed this way but the second answer made the first one pale by comparison. The wagon train carried the dread epidemic. The doctor, fearful and uncertain, had made them keep to their wagons, but his precautions hadn't been enough. Even more chilling, it was entirely possible that they were still unaware that they carried the plague. The mission of mercy had just become a hunt of desperation. His thoughts returned to Melita. "Why did Mexico Jack lie about the wagons stopping here?" he asked.

"I don't know," she said.

"Where'd he go?" Fargo questioned. Her face grew sullen again.

"I can't remember," she said.

"Tell me, goddammit. You know," Fargo said, his eyes cold as an ice floe suddenly, his hand closing around her wrist.

But her almost-black eyes flashed defiance. "I want to leave here. Take me and my memory might come back," she said.

"He made you his woman when you were hardly a woman and you stayed. Why do you want to leave now?" Fargo said.

"I always wanted to leave. I couldn't," she said. Fargo swore under his breath. She could help him but she could also be a problem. She was fifteen years old but twice that in experience, the body of a girl and the soul of a jaded realist who had probably never known childhood. He'd bet on the realist winning out again.

"I can't take you now," Fargo said.

She frowned back. "Why not?"

"He would come to take you back. You know he would and I can't have that now. When it's all over, I'll come back for you. That's the best I can do. Help me now and I'll help you later," he said, waiting as she turned the options over in her mind. "Where did he go, Melita?" he pressed.

Her shoulders dropped. "He went to see Shepley Reisner," she said. "He's a very rich man but he's no good, a real *villano*. Mexico Jack is always bringing him ways to make money and he pays Jack a piece of it."

"Where does he live?"

"North, the way you went but you turn east at the twisted trees," she said.

"I saw them." Fargo nodded. "Now, again, why did Mexico Jack lie about the wagons coming this way?"

"I don't know," Melita said, and this time he believed her. But Mexico Jack had a reason and it was time to find out what. "You will come back for me?" Melita called as he climbed onto the pinto.

"Yes," he said and saw that the hands still lingered at the corral. He put the horse into a canter and saw the day drawing to a close. The night came before he reached the two twisted junipers and he halted, wrestling with decisions. Caroline would stay, he was certain, even if he didn't return by morning. She'd fume at the passage of time but she'd wait. She knew there'd be nothing gained by aimless wandering. He moved the horse on, followed the land east, and the moon was up when he came upon the large house, stables and bunkhouse behind it.

A lamp burned dimly inside the bunkhouse, but the light in the main house reached brightly into the night. Fargo dismounted, left the Ovaro under the branches of a lone black maple, and crept forward. Just outside the main house he found a small shed that let him take cover behind it as well as see into the window. The room he scanned was richly furnished, a deep leather sofa, thick Indian blankets as wall hangings, fine objects of brass, copper, and wood placed on polished furniture. Definitely a wealthy man's house. The figure came into view as he watched. Shepley Reisner was a solidly built man wearing a dark blue smoking jacket. He half turned to show a heavy face with thick, black brows, a long jaw, a face that would have been imperious if it weren't so self-satisfied. He took a long pull of a thick black cigar and gazed out the window at the other side of the room, moved to the leather sofa, and stretched out on it.

He smoked, short, impatient puffs, toyed with reading

a book, rose, paced the room, and gazed out the window again before returning to the sofa. Mexico Jack was nowhere about and Shepley Reisner was a man waiting impatiently. No simple coincidence, no chance juxtaposition of events, Fargo decided, sinking down on one knee and leaning against the shed. It was a time to wait. And to see.

5

Fargo let the passage of the moon across the sky mark
the hours as they slid into one another. The waiting game
was taking its toll. Inside the house, Shepley Reisner
was growing increasingly restless and outside Fargo felt
himself growing increasingly apprehensive. Only the
night concealed him, he realized. He'd have to leave before dawn came or be discovered and he cursed as the
moon began to move down the far end of the trackless
blue ceiling. His lips were a tight line when the sound
came to him and he rose to his feet at once. No single
horse, as he had expected, but at least a half dozen.
More, he corrected himself as the riders drew closer.

He watched through the window as Shepley Reisner
finally heard the sound and went to the door at once.
Fargo stayed against the shed as the riders came into
view, a dark mass, but he guessed there were at least
eight. Reisner had the door open and the horsemen rode
into the square of light that reached out into the night.
Mexico Jack was the first to halt and dismount. Four of
the other riders held boxes in front of them on the saddle
and as Fargo watched, others dismounted, took the
boxes, and carried them into the room, placing them on
the big oak table. Fargo almost winced as he recognized
the boxes. "Tend to your horses and four of you come

back," Reisner told the men as they left. He then turned his attention to the boxes. Mexico Jack untied the first one. Pulling the top open, he brought out a small cardboard box, opened it and pulled out the vial.

Holding the vial aloft, he twirled it in his fingers. "They call it serum. I call it hard cash, jewelry, gold, anything you want," he said. Fargo felt his hand twitch and he had to keep it from going to the Colt at his side. The terrible question tore at him when he suddenly had it answered.

"They put up a fight?" Shepley Reisner asked.

"No, we took 'em by surprise. The washed-out blonde tried to claw me but I flattened her. The rest were all too scared to move." Mexico Jack laughed. Fargo let out a breath of relief and was grateful for that much. He watched as Reisner took out another of the small boxes, extracted the vial of serum from it, and held it up to the light. "Life and death," Mexico Jack said. "They'll beg you to take all their money and anything else they have. No bargaining, believe me. Be like taking candy from a baby, only easier."

"Beautiful," Reisner said, putting the vial back into its box and the box into the larger one. "I figure two, three thousand in cash alone," he said. "Nobody holds back when their life's at stake."

"It won't be just the Turner wagons. Any train you meet will pay whatever you want for the serum once they know smallpox is around," Mexico Jack said and a smile of malicious anticipation spread across Reisner's heavy face. After retying the outer box, he went to a drawer in the table, pulled out a wad of bills, and handed them to Mexico Jack.

"As usual, you bring me a good thing and you get your piece up front, Jack," the man said. Fargo swore silently, the relationship between the two men suddenly clarified. The mutuality of the unscrupulous. Reisner had the money and the organization, Mexico Jack had avenues and opportunities. One hand washed the other and neither had any problem with getting blood on them. "See me next time you have something," Reisner called as Mexico Jack left and the four men returned. "Take the boxes to the shed. They can stay there till we're ready to move out," Reisner ordered, and the men began to pick up the boxes. *Shit,* Fargo swore under his breath, casting a frantic glance around him. There was too much open space. They might glimpse him as he ran. Spinning, he went to the back of the shed, flattened himself against the rear wall, and held his breath, one hand on the butt of the Colt. He listened to the men as they made two trips with the boxes, managing to draw in a deep breath in between trips. He stayed, not moving, until he heard the footsteps move away toward the bunkhouse.

He drew in another deep breath and edged his way around the shed in time to see Shepley Reisner turn out the light inside the house. His lips drawn back, he let his thoughts whirl through him like sagebrush blown in a high wind. Stealing the serum back was the simplest part, and of little use in and of itself. Somebody would check on the boxes, find the serum gone, and they'd conclude only one thing. Reisner would come riding hard to take it back and have no problem following wagon tracks. This time there'd be a pitched gun battle, more of a one-sided slaughter, Fargo swore, with Reisner having eight, maybe ten or twelve gun hands. His lips drew back in a grimace. There was only one answer. He had to steal the serum back but without them knowing it. That was the only way they could get the serum and buy time.

But taking the vials and retying the outer boxes wouldn't be enough. They'd know the vials were gone the minute they lifted one of the boxes. He cursed again and the frown dug into his brow so hard it hurt as he wrestled with one scheme after another. But finally one thought took shape, wild and almost impossible, yet it was all he could put together. He cast a glance up at the moon in the distant sky and guessed that he had perhaps two hours at most. Two hours would have to do, he told himself as he slid away from the shed. He hurried back and retrieved the Ovaro. The light had gone out in the bunkhouse as well as the main house as he walked the Ovaro back to the shed. But as he did, he paused every few paces to gather stones and put them into his saddle-bag. When he reached the shed, one side of his saddle hung low with stones.

From the other side, he took extra shirts out, tied the arms together until he had formed each into a sack, then he did the same with the shirt he took from his back. He went to the shed and carefully began to remove each vial from its small cardboard box until he had one shirt pouch filled. Working silently and quickly, he finally had each shirt filled with the vials and set them on the ground. He began to fill each small box with stones, the task more maddeningly slow than he had anticipated. With each glance skyward he saw the night disappearing.

He found himself cursing silently with each stone he dropped into a box but he held to the task and finally every one of the small boxes was filled. Carefully, he placed them back inside the large boxes. Leaving the door of the shed open to allow the last of the moonlight to filter inside, he moved the large boxes into the shed and retied each one. Finally, he lifted each and allowed a silent grunt of satisfaction. They felt as though they were filled with the bottles of serum. Closing the door to the shed, he picked up the serum vials in the shirt pouches he had formed and put everything into his saddlebags. As he walked the Ovaro from beside the shed, he saw the last of the moon vanish below the horizon. He forced himself to stay at a walk for another hundred yards before climbing into the saddle. He held the horse to a walk, and finally went into a slow trot, riding westward until he found the twisted junipers.

He turned south as the first pink edge of dawn touched the sky. Holding to the slow trot, he kept a steady pace, but the sun was high when he finally reached the break in the junipers. The wagons were exactly where he'd left them. The figures turned to him almost as one as he rode to a halt, but Caroline moved more quickly than the others, rushing to him with a mixture of despair and anger in her face. Her delicate coloring deepened, he saw, as she flung words at him. "Where have you been? The serum's gone, taken from us," she said.

"I know," Fargo said, sliding from the saddle and Caroline's mouth fell open.

"You know?" she gasped.

"The serum is in my saddlebags," he said as the others came to stare at him.

"I don't understand," Caroline said.

"I was at the right place at the right time," Fargo said and explained further in short, terse sentences. He recounted everything that had happened except finding the graves at the way station. It was not something they needed to know yet.

"What a story," Holly said.

"We can go on now," Caroline said.

"You were going to turn back?" Fargo asked with some surprise.

"Without the serum there was no point in going on," Caroline said. "We'd only be empty-handed with nothing to offer. What good would that do?"

"Not much, I guess," Fargo admitted, and his eyes went to Holly.

"We were going on, no matter what," she said, and he caught the faint edge of superiority in her tone. So did Caroline.

"Touching," she said, then spun and snapped orders at Burt Hobbs to help take the serum from the saddlebags. Fargo studied Holly for a moment, and Randi beside her, and he had to wonder if it really was friendship that spurred her determination. She was still a question mark. He grunted and turned away to watch as Caroline had the vials packed into blankets and sheets and put in a corner of the wagon, where they'd be wedged in tightly.

"We'll ride into the night," he said.

"You think they'll be coming after us?" Ben asked.

"If they think they have the serum they'll be searching to find the Turner train. If they find out the serum's not there they'll sure as hell come after us," Fargo said.

"How would they find that out?" Holly queried.

"Lots of ways. A box could come untied and somebody look inside. They might drop a box and look inside. Or they could meet a wagon train and offer the serum and find out all they have is rocks. I'm not taking chances. I want to make time," Fargo said. He checked inside Caroline's wagon and found her facing him, the pale blue eyes searching his face.

"Thanks to you, we still have a chance to save a lot of people," she said. "I can't thank you enough, not really." Her hands came to rest against his chest and suddenly her lips were on his, a quick, fleeting touch, soft as a butterfly's wing.

"That's a start," he said. She answered with a very serious, unsmiling nod and stepped back. He swung down from the wagon and walked to where Ben Smith adjusted the harness on the right mare. Ben's crinkly face peered up at him with an added crinkle.

"What happens when they catch up to us?" Ben asked.

"You sound like you expect they will," Fargo said.

"Don't you?" Ben grunted.

Fargo allowed a wry snort. "Still being an old fox, aren't you?" he muttered and the old codger waited. "I don't know," Fargo admitted. "I'm still working on it."

"Keep thinking," Ben said and Fargo climbed onto the Ovaro and sent the horse forward. He rode with his lips in a tight line. Maybe he'd have no answer, he realized. Catching up to the Turner wagons was growing even more important and he wasn't sure why. He glanced back, saw the others following, and led the way along an uneven passage that stayed open and firm as the day ended and night bore down. When the moon finally touched the top of the sky, he called a halt and bedded down. He had everyone riding when the new day broke.

When he came onto a wide stream, he halted. As the others filled canteens and watered the horses, he walked ahead with the Ovaro following, his eyes peering hard at the land near the stream. The location fitted, the place was right, and his trailsman's eyes read the ground as other men read books. Grama grass lay low to the ground. Rising higher, thick growths of sweet clover waved with their tall, delicate yellow buds. He studied the grama grass first. The older stalks were leaning into each other, and next to them the newer ones pushed up straight. His eyes moved to the sweet clover and he saw the faint bruising along the bottoms of the stalks. It was another small sign to Fargo and he carefully parted the clover, then the grama grass, and allowed a smile of triumph as the marks appeared—wagon wheels that ran one behind the other. Once again, time and nature had combined to keep their secrets and once again, the Trailsman had pierced their silent conspiracy.

He rose and shouted, waving the others forward. Then he mounted the Ovaro and set a fast pace, confident now that he had no need to spend time searching for wagon tracks. They had come this way and he had only to follow the natural paths the Turner wagons would have taken. Before night fell, the wagon tracks came clearly into sight and he halted, dropped to the ground, and let his fingers crumble the edges of the tracks. There was still dampness clinging to the ridges. They were moving closer, he noted in satisfaction. "How soon," Holly asked when they halted to bed down for the night. "I saw you examining the tracks."

"Can't say for sure. Some days more, but we're catching up," he told her and saw the touch of satisfaction come into her face.

"And the others who might be coming after us?" she asked. "Think they've gone their way?"

"No," he said and saw the satisfaction turn into apprehension.

"Maybe we ought to move night and day, only rest a few hours," Holly suggested.

"Your Percherons might do it, not the other horses," he said.

She stepped closer, her hands on his chest. "The hell with the other horses and you get a bonus you'll never forget," she said.

"I'll do my best," he said, and she hurried away. He

had gone off by himself and set out his bedroll, when Caroline appeared.

"What was that all about?" she asked.

"Anybody tell you it's not polite to spy on people?" he asked mildly.

"Wasn't spying. Just happened to see her go to you," Caroline said, sounding hurt.

"She's worried, anxious, and concerned for her friend," Fargo said.

"That goes for all of us," Caroline said.

"Guess so," he agreed, and suddenly her mouth was against his, no fleeting touch this time but lingering warmth until she pulled away.

"I wouldn't want you giving her special treatment," Caroline said with sudden primness.

"Wouldn't think of it," Fargo said and she hurried away. He finished undressing, and as he lay down on the bedroll he wondered whether when it was all over Caroline might be the most surprising of all. He slept quickly, woke early, and again set a fast pace that led onto a high plain with a good covering of gambel oak. He left the wagons to ride onto higher ground and let his eyes sweep the land below. A spiral of dust caught his eye and he rode forward until the dust led him to five Conestogas crossing from north to south in a single line. He moved the pinto downhill and came alongside the lead wagon, which was driven by a pleasant-faced man in overalls. A woman with her hair piled high in a bun sat beside him. He noted towheaded kids and other families in the following wagons.

"'Morning, friend. Jed Hopkins, here. My wife, Sadie," the man said.

"Wonder if you might have come onto a train of nine wagons heading west," Fargo asked.

"We did," the man said. "We were going to stop a spell and break bread when we crossed paths. But we didn't."

Something in the man's voice made Fargo peer at him. "Why not?" he asked.

"There was a doctor with them. He rode out to meet us, stayed a way back as he talked. He said they might have smallpox on their train. We were real beholden to him for telling us," Jed Hopkins said. "We turned and gave them a wide berth. We've heard how catching that is."

"Nothing like being careful about epidemics," Fargo agreed, letting thoughts tumble through his head for a moment. "If some riders come by and offer you smallpox serum, tell them you're not interested," he said.

"Why in hell would we do that?" The man frowned.

"Heard that they were selling fake serum," Fargo said. "Just tell them you've got your own serum and go your way."

"Damn, what people won't stoop to," the man said. "Thanks for telling us."

"My pleasure," Fargo said and put the pinto into a trot. Maybe he had bought a little more time, he told himself. If Reisner was turned aside he'd have no reason to bring out the serum and find the truth of what he had. It was a long shot, Fargo realized, but the entire mission was more and more getting to seem a long shot. He didn't return to the hills and instead crossed to where Caroline and the others moved slowly under a hot sun.

"They could all use a rest," Ben Smith said to him, nodding to those following. Fargo's eyes moved across the others. They were all showing the effects of the sun, including Burt Hobbs's men. Harry Adamson was perhaps perspiring the most, his face flushed. He had removed his jacket but his hair remained in place. Fargo's eyes went to the horses. They were in less distress than the riders.

"They can rest when we bed down," he said to Ben and rode ahead, aware that he'd been unfeeling. But the meeting with the Conestogas had filled him with foreboding and he motioned for them to follow along a path where the wagon tracks were clear. He rode forward and when the path opened onto a wide plain he saw the sun nearing the horizon. He also saw the four objects that rose from the ground a few hundred feet ahead. He grimaced as the conclusion instantly struck him. He hoped against hope but an inner sense told him hope was an empty exercise. For a moment, he considered leading the others in a sharp turn, but then he realized they were too close.

And perhaps there was nothing to be gained. Perhaps it was not a time for sparing. They came up behind him as he reined to a halt and waited, dismounting to stare at the stone and wood markers. They had been carefully but crudely erected and he heard Caroline's gasp, then the murmur that coursed through the others. He squatted, reading the names that had been cut into a length of bark and fitted among the stones: ED OSGOOD, BETH OSGOOD, JIMMY AND BILLY. CAME TOGETHER. DIED TOGETHER.

Caroline's voice came first. "Oh, my God. There's no more wondering now," she said.

"Shit," Randi bit out. "That does it. They're probably all dead by now."

"No," Caroline said sharply. "It could've just hit this family."

"Stop kiddin' yourself," Randi threw back. "Smallpox is a goddamn plague and plagues wipe out everybody."

"Shut up," Holly hissed at her. "We're going on, dammit."

"I sure as hell am," Harry Adamson said.

"Me, too. Can't desert my friend Orrin, even if he's dead," Ernie Alden put in.

"I want to see about Aaron and Bettie for myself," Herb Baxter said.

"I want to go on, too. I just think we must be realistic," Caroline said. "I hope there are some the serum can still save."

"Enough goddamn talk. I'll ride till midnight," Holly said. "Let's go."

Fargo half shrugged and waved them forward, bringing the pinto alongside Caroline as she sat beside Ben on the wagon. "They're all more dedicated to their friends than I expected they would be," she said.

"Maybe," he grunted and drew a quick glance from her.

"Meaning what?" she asked, keeping her voice low though Holly's wagon plodded a dozen feet behind.

"They seem more determined than dedicated," he remarked.

"What makes you say that?" she asked.

"I heard anger, exasperation, frustration. I didn't hear any sympathy. You were the only one upset," Fargo said.

"You don't miss much, do you?" Caroline said.

"That's why you came to me, isn't it?" he returned and she nodded, a wry admiration in the pale blue eyes. The day began to fade and quickly became night. Fargo stayed on the high plains, certain it was the way the Turner wagons had gone. A gnawing apprehension grew inside him as he rode. Reisner and his men would be catching up within another day or two, he guessed, and the question remained: did they know they were carrying rocks? Fargo frowned into the night, aware that he hadn't yet come up with a way to be prepared for the answer. Perhaps it was that double-edged fact that made him keep the wagons rolling until the moon had passed the midnight sky.

He finally found a small dip in the land with a thick forest of red cedar. After bringing the others into the protection of the trees, he had them pull the wagons deep into the foliage. They ate cold beef strips, some talked in low murmurs. Caroline kept to herself. When the others bedded down, Fargo took his bedroll a dozen yards away, but stayed inside the forest, gratefully embracing sleep as the night stayed quiet. When the pink of the new day touched the land, seeping slowly into the forest, he woke. After pulling on his clothes, he scanned the forest, where most of the others were still clinging to sleep.

A figure moved and he saw it was Ben Smith. Trousers on and holding a shirt, Ben came toward him. "She's gone," he said, and Fargo frowned back. "Caroline. I heard her get up a little before daybreak. I sat up and she said she couldn't sleep and was going to take a little walk. I went back to sleep but I looked for her just now and she's nowhere around."

"Damn fool girl," Fargo hissed. He stepped to the edge of the cedar forest and peered out to the open land beyond. "I don't like it," he muttered.

"What's the matter?" Holly's voice asked, and he turned to see her by her wagon, a nightdress hardly concealing her full contours.

"Caroline's missing. I'm going to look for her. Maybe she just got herself lost," he said. "Everybody stays here in the forest. Anyone passes by you stay low and keep the horses quiet." He paused and peered at her. "You know how to keep a horse quiet, don't you?" he asked.

She half shrugged. "Hold him in one place. Hold his mouth shut so he won't blow air," she said.

"That'll make it worse," he said. "You keep a horse quiet by stroking him, calming him."

"I'll see to it," Ben said, and Fargo strode to the Ovaro and took the rifle from its saddle case. He reached down and pulled the double-edged throwing knife from the holster on his calf and walked from the forest, the Ovaro at his heels. He found Caroline's footprints quickly. She had wandered aimlessly, pausing often only to go on again. Her prints moved into clusters of crested wheat-grass, then large thickets of delicate yellow flowering rabbitbrush.

He pushed his way through the clusters of the rabbitbrush when his lips drew back, his eyes resting on the footprints that were no longer just Caroline's. Six pairs of moccasin prints met his gaze, their smooth, unlined impressions unmistakable. He saw the prints surround those of Caroline's, and how she was pulled along to where he spied the unshod prints of the Indian ponies. The rabbitbrush wore faint edges of bruising where the ponies were led west. Fargo stayed on foot as he followed. Then he slowed as he suddenly heard voices. A growth of sagebrush afforded him cover as he dropped into a crouch and crept closer, pushing the throwing knife closer to the center of his belt. A sharp, half gasp, Caroline's voice, cut the air and he halted, peering forward to where Caroline sat on the ground, a long nightdress half off one shoulder. Six braves surrounded her, pulling at the dress, lifting the bottom edge to look at her beautifully long, tapered legs. She half turned, fighting to pull the dress down.

His eyes went to the armband of one of the braves and he saw the beadwork that marked the designs of the Ute.

The six braves continued to play with Caroline, one moving in, grabbing her arms from behind as she tried to twist away, but only succeeding in showing more of her long legs. Fargo's hand went to the hilt of the throwing knife. He had already decided against gunshots unless he had absolutely no other choice. Shepley Reisner could be close enough to hear. He'd come racing and Fargo didn't want that. Silence, Fargo told himself again as he drew the thin, razor-sharp blade from his belt. He raised his arm and took aim at the Ute holding Caroline by the arms as another near-naked form began to lift her dress. Using all the strength in his powerful arm, he sent the blade whirling through the air.

It smashed into the brave's upper sternum, shattering the bone as it penetrated to the hilt. The man's eyes bulged and his mouth fell open, his breath suddenly a harsh, wheezing sound as he toppled backward. The others were staring at him, transfixed by the sudden explosion of death. But Fargo was already racing forward, the heavy rifle held clublike in his hands. He smashed it into the temple of the nearest Ute and the Indian went down. The brave nearest him began to turn and tried to reach for a scraping knife at his belt, but he closed his fingers around the knife as the rifle butt drove forward into his throat with all Fargo's weight and power behind it. The Ute fell with a terrible, gurgling sound coming from the smashed bones of his larynx. The other three Utes, recovering from their surprise, started toward him, one drawing a tomahawk from a leather holder, the other two coming up with hunting knives.

Fargo saw Caroline, on her feet, leaning over beside the first of Fargo's targets. The three Utes separated to come at him, one directly at him, the other two from each side. He half circled, shifting the heavy rifle in his hands and moving to the left, turning as if he were trying to run. The Ute nearest came in with a rush, his knife raised. Fargo continued to seem to flee. He let the brave come within a foot of him, then he whirled and spun the rifle as though it were a pinwheel. The end of the stock caught the Ute on the point of the jaw and the man staggered backward, his eyes glazing. Fargo spun the rifle again a short arc in the other direction and this time the heavy stock slammed into the Ute's cheekbone. The man's glazed eyes went altogether blank. He started to sink down when the muzzle of the rifle drove a hole into the side of his neck.

Fargo flung himself sideways, twisting as he did, as he felt and heard the other two Indians coming at him. He felt the hunting knife swish past his head as he hit the ground, rolling and coming up on one knee. Out of the corner of his eye, he caught Caroline as she held the thin throwing knife she'd pulled from the dead Ute. She tossed it to him and he caught it with one hand, backtracking furiously as the two remaining Utes came at him again. The one with the hunting knife moved at him first with small, darting steps. Fargo went backward again and suddenly halted and let the Ute charge. With a quick underhand toss, Fargo sent the double-edged blade in a short, upward trajectory. The Ute tried to twist out of the way as he glimpsed the blade hurtling at him. He was only partly successful as the blade smashed into his side. He gasped an oath as he fell to both knees, grabbing at the blade jutting out from between his ribs. Fargo saw him pull it from his ribs and fall sideways to the ground in pain and then Fargo backed up again as the last Indian came at him with his tomahawk. Younger than the others, he seemed little more than a tall boy, but the tomahawk was no toy and the Ute's lips were pulled back in a grimace of determination.

Fargo faced him, holding the rifle as a club once again. The Ute ducked low, came in, feinted, and then let go a quick and vicious swipe with the short-handled axe. The blow missed, but not by much, and Fargo swung a counter blow with the rifle. The youth was quick as the blow went wide. He backed up, and let the Ute come at him again. Then he feinted to his left but the Indian answered with a vicious swipe of the tomahawk. The Ute came at him again, moving from side to side on the balls of his feet, lashing out with a quick, chopping blow that Fargo barely avoided. Fargo ducked away from another fast blow, the tomahawk whistling past his ear. The Ute continued his pressure, swiping and chopping with the weapon, each blow coming closer.

Fargo tried countering and missed as the Ute ducked away. He found himself almost falling as the tomahawk lashed upward to graze his shoulder. The Ute was made of hair-trigger reflexes and one would soon find its mark, Fargo realized. His only chance, besides pulling the trigger, was to trick the Indian into a mistake. He feinted again and almost felt the sharp edge of the tomahawk against his scalp. He backed up and tried another feint, and was met by a short, upward blow of the ax. He kept going backward, letting the Ute think he was trying only to parry blows. The Indian came in with new disregard for his foe. Fargo twisted away from a blow and let himself fall. Then he spun and came up on both knees. The Ute rushed, tomahawk raised, certain he'd bring it down on Fargo's head. He would have, without a question, if Fargo had tried to push to his feet. But Fargo let himself go forward, staying low and swinging the heavy rifle in a flat arc, crashing it into the Ute's kneecaps.

The Indian let out a shout of pain as his knees collapsed under him and he went down. Fargo, on one knee, brought the stock of the rifle smashing down onto the Ute's jaw with all the force in his powerful arms and shoulders. He heard the man's neck snap as his head turned almost completely around. With a silent curse, Fargo used the rifle to help himself push to his feet and he saw Caroline looking on, her face almost colorless. She came toward him and fell into his arms as she murmured into his chest. "You did it . . . got all of them. I didn't believe you could do it," she said.

"You helped some," he said as he led her to the Ovaro, pausing to retrieve the thin throwing knife.

"Why didn't you shoot? You out of bullets?" she asked.

"Shots make noise," he said, swinging her onto the Ovaro with him. "Wandering around was a pretty dumb thing to do."

"Couldn't sleep and then I got lost. I lay down to wait for sunup, only they came with the sun," she said.

"Next time you can't sleep come see me," he said gruffly.

She half turned in the saddle and he felt her hand rest on his thigh. "Yes," she said, not smiling, her face very grave. "Yes." He rode back to the cedar forest, where the others were waiting and not hiding their impatience.

"More time wasted," Holly said.

"I'm sorry," Caroline said, taking in everyone with a glance.

"Can we get going now?" Harry Adamson said petulantly and Fargo nodded. Caroline went inside the wagon and dressed as Ben drove from the cedar forest with Fargo riding alongside. Fargo set a brisk pace across the relatively open land, staying west as he followed the tracks of the Turner wagons. He left the others twice to ride up onto a low hill that let him peer back the way they had come. With no signs of riders coming along behind, he allowed himself both satisfaction and uneasiness, satisfaction because they had gained another day, and uneasiness because he knew they were on borrowed time. He kept the wagons rolling after night fell, but when the land became a series of ravines and juniper-covered plateaus the wagon tracks grew unreadable. He called a halt at the front edge of a wide ravine where a thick stand of mountain mahogany grew, the tree that was not really a tree but a treelike shrub. It afforded a good place for the wagons to nestle and the horses to forage.

Fargo took his bedroll off to the distant edges of the thick growth, where he saw that many of the branches were covered by the two-inch white plumes that meant seeds were ready to fall. He undressed, lay down, and slept quickly until the morning came. When he finished dressing and went to the wagons he saw Holly's big hay wagon nose-down on the ground, the others standing around it. He saw the broken wheel as he came closer and Holly's eyes went to him at once. "I've an extra wheel. I've just got to put it on," she said.

"We'll help her," Burt Hobbs said.

"It just gave way, knocked me off the mattress," Randi said.

"It happens," Fargo said, bent down to examine the wheel. The wood had simply split and given way.

"I figure we can get a new wheel on in a couple of hours. Main problem will be lifting this baby. She's a heavy one," Burt Hobbs said.

Fargo straightened up, letting his eyes go to the wide ravine that stretched out alongside the uneven high land.

He saw the wagon tracks amid the gray-green sagebrush and let his gaze go to the horizon line where the ravine ended. "Follow the ravine," he told Holly. "I'm going to ride the high land ahead. I'll meet up with you later."

"One damn delay after another," Harry Adamson grumbled, turning away as Fargo climbed onto the Ovaro. He saw Caroline watching him.

"I could go on alone," she said.

"No. Keep your wagons together. I don't want to have to look for two of you," Fargo said, turning the horse and moving onto the uneven, tree-studded land that rose above the ravine as it paralleled the wide valley. He searched to find a shortcut to the Turner train, perhaps a pass that would let him go where the wagons couldn't follow. If so, he'd transfer the serum to saddlebags to make up time. But first he had to find that shortcut and he stayed at a slow trot along the high land, cursing as he saw nothing that would help cut time and distance. He circled thick clusters of junipers and made his way through tangles of rabbitbrush and mountain mahogany. Finally halting to rest, his eyes swept the land that stretched ahead.

He dismounted and sat on the ground under the hot sun when his ears, always tuned for any sudden sound, picked up hoofbeats, a single horse moving slowly. He rose to one knee, his hand immediately on the butt of the Colt at his side. Peering through the brush, he saw the horse and rider push into sight, the rider's light blond hair even yellower in the sun. He rose to his feet and dropped his hand from the Colt as Caroline halted and slid from the saddle. "Used one of the extra horses," she said. "Told Ben to drive when they were ready and I'd meet him later."

"Thought you'd learned a lesson about wandering around alone," Fargo said.

"Wasn't wandering. I followed your tracks," Caroline said.

"Why? Couldn't stand waiting around?" he asked.

"That was part of it," she said.

"What was the other part?"

She took a step forward and suddenly her arms were around his neck, her mouth pressing his in a long, soft kiss. "This," she murmured, stepping back. In the bright, hot sun, her pale blue eyes seemed almost colorless, yet they retained their strange, pale intensity, not unlike a fire that seemed to blaze without flame. Her lips in the burning sun, already a pale pink, were almost colorless, her skin the delicate white of a porcelain teacup. "Surprised?" she asked.

"Yes," he admitted.

"That makes two of us," she said as her arms slid around his neck again.

6

Her lips clung again, so very soft yet so simmeringly anxious. When she pulled back he saw the pale-fire eyes studying his, her face unsmiling. She wore a dark blue dress that was one piece. A few quick motions with her hands and the garment slid from her to land at her feet. Fargo felt his breath draw in sharply at the naked loveliness of her as she stood very straight, as if offering herself for his approval and at the same time taunting him with her beauty.

He saw the skin of her body echoed that of her face, all a seamless, delicate white porcelain teacup that almost glowed. Her breasts, slightly shallow and very modest, nonetheless fit perfectly on the long slenderness of her body. His eyes went to the nipples that were a faint pink, the areolas around each so pale as to be almost colorless. Yet for all the pale delicacy of her, all the fragile coloration, she somehow exuded a pastel vibrancy, that remarkable combination of delicacy and strength that made him think of an Easter lily.

A small waist curved deliciously inward to add to the slender beauty of her, and her long legs tapered beautifully, thighs narrow yet shapely, calves smooth and long-lined. Just below a flat, almost concave abdomen, a jet-black, bushy nap was startlingly incongruous with the translucent white-porcelain of her skin. He brought her down to a carpet of star moss, shedding his own clothes and she came to him, pressing herself tight against him, body to body, and he felt her tremble. "Oh, oh . . . oh, my God," Caroline breathed, rubbing herself against him, trembling in pleasure again, reveling in the tactile. Her hands moved across his shoulders, back and forth, down to his chest, and little sighing sounds came from her. "Nice . . . oh, so nice, so good," she murmured, and he felt her teeth against one shoulder, half biting, half nibbling. His mouth moved down, sliding across the shallow curve of one breast, finding the pale pink tip. Caroline uttered a tiny cry. Then she gasped and arched her back as she pushed her breast upward. "Yes, oh my God, yes . . . yes, more, more," she murmured, and he drew in more of the soft little mound, letting his tongue trace a lambent path around the pastel pink circle. Caroline cried out, a fervent gasp, and he saw her torso twist to one side, then the other, her long, slender legs clasped tightly together as they swung back and forth. The white porcelain skin had taken on faint color, he saw, a kind of suffused rose that gave her a warm vibrancy.

His hands slid downward over her slender body, exploring smooth curves and little mounds. He touched, caressed and fondled her, enjoying the smoothness of her while listening to the tiny murmurs of pleasure that came from her lips in soft sighs, quick gasps, and long moans. As his lips moved to her body, they pursued their own incandescent paths. Gasps became small cries and cries became half screams. "My God, oh, yes, yes, yes . . . oh, God, yes," Caroline breathed, and the delicate rose of her skin became a deeper pink. He touched the jet-black, bushy nap and her torso jerked upward, twisted, and rose again. He pressed down and was surprised at the firm roundness of her Venus mound and touched the faint dampness of the villous patch. His hand slid further, touching the skin of her thighs and her sweet moistness. Caroline's fingers dug into his shoulders. She brought her slender body around and pressed her Venus mound into his pulsating erectness. She half screamed at the touch.

Her rose-tinted thighs fell open, closed, and fell open again, and when they closed again his hand was against the tip of her dark, warm portal. Caroline shuddered, gasped out words: "Yes, yes, touch me, touch me, take me, do me . . . oh, God, yes." Suddenly the rose-tinted delicacy of her, the pastel beauty of her, was soft steel, that quiet strength that lay just beneath the porcelain exterior. It had hinted at itself before and now it took command. Her hand came to his, pressed him to her, and guided his fingers along the overwhelming sensations of her honeyed halls. "Yes, oh, God, oh, God, yes," Caroline breathed and he felt the softness of long thighs coming to clasp around him, moving, turning, seeking, wanting. He let her portal find him and heard her long, shuddering moan of pure ecstasy as he slid into her.

She moved at once, long, slow, heaving motions, setting rhythm, pace, sensual command, and he let her, joined with her. She half sobbed and half laughed, sensations too strong to hold in check, too consuming to command. He felt her tightness around him, throbbing, caressing, returning touch for touch, pleasure for pleasure. She pushed the smallish breasts into his mouth, arms and legs wrapped around him until she seemed no longer a separate person but melded together with him, forever and inextricably entwined. She was screaming now, screams of ecstasy with every turn and twist, proving the strength of delicate things. Her cries grew higher, tighter, and he could feel the urgency begin to sweep through her as her slender body clung, rubbing, twisting, sliding, lifting. He caught a glimpse of her eyes, saw that they were a pale fire that seemed almost unearthly, so colorless yet so powerful, so pale yet so wild, a fire that was without flame yet burned so hotly.

As he watched her, he saw her lips moving, a kind of disbelief seizing her face. "Now, now, oh, God, now . . . aaaaiiiiii," Caroline screamed, digging her heels into the carpet of moss as she almost lifted him into the air. He felt himself swept along with her as she spiraled to that sublime moment of total sensual release and his face buried into the soft, smallish breasts, he heard her cries as from a faraway place, felt her tightness around him, and joined with her in the sheer ecstasy of the senses. Finally, with a long, protesting sigh, her body relaxed against his and the world asserted itself. She lay beside him, drawing in long, deep breaths, and he pushed up on one elbow to enjoy the sheer loveliness of her. Her white-porcelain body was still softly suffused with rose, the faint pink of her nipples an added touch of color, the sun-bleached hay that was her pale crown, all of her once again a picture of delicacy.

Yet he had just seen that quietly powerful part of her, the wildness that could explode all the fragile paleness. Pale fire, he murmured to himself once again, contrasts somehow made one. She stirred, interrupted his thoughts, and came against him, all warm softness. She slid her body upward to press one faint pink nipple against his lips. "I never expected this would happen," she murmured.

"Sometimes it's best that way, unexpected," he said.

"Yes, oh, yes," Caroline agreed with quiet vigorousness and pressed harder into him, bringing the bushy nap against his groin.

"We have to ride," he reminded her gently. She nodded, drew back, and sat up, disappointment in her face.

"And find another place, another time," she said, slipping on clothes.

"Is that an order?" He laughed, dressing.

"Order, invitation, prayer, take your pick," she said and clung to him a moment longer. "I've never been much for omens but maybe this was one," she said, and he frowned back. "That everything will turn out for the best," she said, and he said nothing as he climbed onto the Ovaro. Hope sometimes is best left a silent thing, he told himself. She rode beside him as he continued along the high ground, but finally moved downward to the wide ravine, cursing under his breath. The land had offered no shortcuts, no passes that could cut the time to the Turner train and he had a place to bed down picked out as the wagons finally rolled into sight.

"Feed and water your horses early," he told them. "We go hard and long tomorrow. We're running out of time."

"You mean, if they have smallpox?" Holly asked.

"I mean a dozen gunslingers will be coming after us. Whether there's smallpox or not, we have to get the serum to those wagons before that happens," Fargo said and his grimness reached the others as they turned away in silence. He took his bedroll into a clump of alligator junipers when Caroline appeared and stood close to him. "I'll stay with my omen. Today was too wonderful for anything else," she said gravely.

He drew her to him. She had to believe that, he realized. She didn't dare let herself believe anything else. He'd not take that from her, not until he had no choice. Her strength was really a terrible fear. "Yes, it was wonderful. Now get some sleep," he said. Her lips lingered on his before she hurried away and he lay down on the bedroll, drawing sleep around himself until the new sun finally swept away the night. He rose, washed, and dressed, then walked to where the others prepared to roll. Caroline sat beside Ben Smith; Holly and Randi were already on the driver's seat of their big rig. "Stay in the ravine. I'll be riding ahead. I'll meet with you later," he instructed. "Make time. Rest the horses, not yourselves."

As he passed Ben Smith, the old driver spoke in a barely audible whisper. "You're getting nervous, old friend," he said. Fargo paused, and met his waiting eyes.

"Just between us?" he asked, and Ben nodded. "Yes. Very nervous." Fargo strode to the Ovaro, swung onto the horse, and rode away at a fast canter. He slowed, but held to a steady pace. The wide ravine ran in almost a straight line, the wagon tracks clear and easy to see. He halted frequently to dismount and run his hands across the ruts and ridges, each crumbled piece of soil a word, each touch of moisture or dryness a syllable, until the language of the trail revealed its secrets. The sun had moved into the afternoon when he saw the flatness of the land suddenly broken with a small half mound. He rode forward and the half mound grew more distinct and he heard the bitter oath fall from his lips.

He reined to a halt and swung to the ground to stare at the two, freshly dug graves; crude wooden crosses marked the head of each of them. A wooden headstone had been erected between both mounds, words carved into it with a knife. He knelt down and read the uneven lines aloud: "Efren and Alice Torrance and baby Torrance, who never got to see the world. July 10, 1860." Pushing to his feet, he decided to wait and sat down against the stump of an old black maple. When Caroline's wagon rolled up, he rose and waited as she swung to the ground, her eyes on the graves. Holly and the others came along soon after and it was Randi who broke the silence.

"That does it. They've all got it," she said.

"No, it doesn't always work that way," Caroline snapped. "I told you that."

"Stop trying to kid us," Randi threw back.

"I'm telling you the truth," Caroline insisted. "You never know how a plague such as smallpox will strike. You can't give up now."

"Who said anything about giving up?" Holly cut in, her eyes going to Fargo. "How much longer before we catch up to them?"

"Another day. Maybe two," Fargo said.

"We're that close?" Caroline asked.

"Yes. They've slowed a lot," he answered. Caroline frowned into space for a moment, her lips becoming a thin line, and he watched her fight with herself. Finally, a decision made, she spoke out.

"Maybe it hasn't spread further, but maybe it has. There's only one thing to do. I'll inoculate one person who can go on ahead, and see the situation and then report back to us," she said.

"Why one person? Inoculate all of us, dammit," Holly snapped.

"Not until I find out how much serum they'll be needing. Inoculating everyone here could make us run short. They might need double doses," Caroline countered, reaching into her wagon for one of the vials of serum and a hypodermic syringe. "I'll inoculate Fargo. He'll make the best time and give a good report on what he finds," she said and stepped to where Fargo looked on.

She filled the syringe with the contents of the vial as he pushed up one sleeve. "This will give the serum overnight, maybe twenty-four hours, to work before you reach the wagons." She had one hand on his arm, deciding the best spot to inject the needle, when the voice cut in.

"No. Hold it right there." Fargo turned to see Harry Adamson holding a pistol aimed at Caroline. "You'll inoculate me. I'm going." Fargo eyed the gun, saw it was a five-shot, double-action Remington-Rider, not a fast weapon with a slow hammer speed and stiff trigger pull. "Come on, get over here with it," Adamson ordered Caroline.

Fargo's eyes narrowed at the man. "Why, Adamson? You're not that concerned over your friend. What's the real reason?" he probed.

"Just give me the damn inoculation," Adamson snarled and raised the pistol at Caroline. "I'm getting to those wagons first."

Fargo saw Caroline's helpless glance at him. He kept his voice even. "Do what the man says. He's in a real big hurry. He wants speed. Get at it," Fargo said. Caroline hesitated and then the flare of understanding came into the pale-fire eyes. She stepped over to Harry Adamson and the man poked the Remington-Rider into her ribs as she pushed up his sleeve.

Fargo's hand had stolen up to the butt of the Colt at his side and his eyes were boring into Harry Adamson. There'd be a moment if Caroline did her part, only a split second, but it would be enough. His body steel-wire tight, Fargo watched Caroline pause, then jab the needle hard into Adamson's arm. The man flinched in pain and, for a moment his gun wavered and left Caroline's ribs. Fargo's hand was already yanking the Colt from its holster and firing as the barrel came up. Adamson cursed in pain as the pistol flew from his hand and Fargo was at his side instantly as Caroline spun out of the way. Fargo pressed the Colt to Adamson's temple, the man's face going ashen with fear and pain as he held his one hand with the other. "Now talk, mister. Why do you have to get to the Turner wagons so badly?" Fargo said. "What's Burton the banker to you, the truth of it?"

"We worked at the Nebraska State Bank together. We embezzled a lot of money. We were going to take off together with it," Adamson said.

"Only he decided to go it alone with all of the money," Fargo finished.

"Cheating bastard. He won't get away with it. Dead or alive, he's not keeping that money," Adamson said.

"But now you'll wait like everybody else," Fargo said.

"Only we're not waiting," Holly's voice interrupted. "She's going to inoculate us."

Fargo kept the barrel of the Colt against Adamson's temple as his eyes went to Holly. She stood beside Randi, who held an old Walken plains rifle pressed into Caroline's back. "Don't try anything like you did with him," Holly said almost chidingly. "She won't be the first person Randi's shot."

Fargo's lips pursed, but he kept the Colt against Adamson's temple. "She pulls that trigger and I pull this one," Fargo said.

"No, Jesus . . . no," Adamson said, his voice cracking.

"Looks as though we have a standoff," Fargo said evenly.

"Wrong," Holly said, and Fargo frowned back at her.

"How do you figure that?" he asked.

"You don't want to see Miss Caroline dead but I don't

108

give a shit if you blow his head off," Holly returned. "No standoff."

"Bitch," Adamson spit out.

Holly shrugged. "Still no standoff. You put down your gun, Fargo, and she inoculates us and we're on our way. No more talk," she said coldly.

The voice interrupted. "That's right. No more talk and no standoff." Fargo's eyes flicked to his left to see Ben Smith holding a heavy army carbine aimed at Randi. "Never shot a woman before. Hate to make this a first," the old driver said.

"Goddamn," Holly hissed as Randi lowered the rifle.

"Drop it," Ben ordered and Randi let the rifle fall to the ground. Fargo took the Colt from Adamson's head and the man sank to one knee as he drew in deep gasps of breath.

"How about the truth from you girls?" Fargo said, facing Holly as Randi and Terry Jones flanked her. "You never were schoolteachers. I'd guess saloon girls," he said.

"Good-enough guess." Holly half shrugged.

"Your friend Lila Tomkins with the Turner wagons, she's one of you," Fargo said.

"Another good guess," Holly said.

"Why are you chasing her?" Fargo questioned.

"Guess it's not so different from Adamson," Holly said. "We pooled our money to go into business for ourselves, buy our own place. She ran off with everything, the bitch. She's not getting away with it."

Fargo turned to where Ernie Alden and Herb Baxter looked on, the Colt still in his hand. "Let's get it all out in the open," he said. "You're no traveling salesman, Ernie, and I'll bet that Orrin Dodge is no lumberman. What's your story?"

"I invented an attachment that makes it easier to plow rough ground. Orrin Dodge backed me, then he took the drawings and had them patented in his name. I want that patent. It's my invention. He's not running off with it, the thieving bastard," Ernie Alden said.

"You've a gun someplace. Save me the trouble of searching for it," Fargo said.

"A pistol, in my saddlebag," the younger man said.

"Get it, carefully," Fargo said, watching while Ernie Alden brought a seven-shot, single-action Smith & Wesson. Fargo took it and handed it to Ben as he turned to the thin, balding figure of Herb Baxter. "That leaves you," he said. Herb Baxter's face held a strange mixture of emotions as he answered with righteousness, bitterness, anger, and embarrassment.

"Bettie's my wife. She and Aran Stillman ran off together, made a laughingstock out of me. They won't get away with it. They're going to pay," the man said, his voice tight.

Fargo frowned at him. "You're figuring to kill at least one of them, aren't you?" he said.

"That's what they deserve," the man snarled.

"I don't think the law approves of that kind of divorce," Fargo said. "Let's have the gun." Herb Baxter went to his horse and handed over a Colt army pistol.

"You can't take our guns. We may be needing them later," Baxter protested.

"You'll get them back, then," Fargo said, his eyes hard as they swept over the figures in front of him. "You're some collection. Caroline's the only one of you on a mission of mercy. The rest of you are all more anxious to kill than to save. None of you have clean hands."

"My invention was stolen" Ernie Alden said.

"So you say," Fargo returned.

"I'm a wronged husband," Herb Baxter said.

"Maybe and maybe she had good reason to run away," Fargo shot back. "I don't know and I don't care but I'll be going to the wagons first." He beckoned to Caroline, who came to him with the hypodermic needle and the others watched in truculent silence as she gave him the injection of serum. When she was through, he helped Ben put the guns into her wagon as dusk began to drop over the land. "We'll bed down here," he said curtly and the others moved away, Holly and the two young women going to the big hay wagon.

"They'll try again during the night," Ben said quietly as he stood beside Fargo and Caroline. "They're all determined and they won't just give up. What do we do, stand guard over Caroline?"

"They want the inoculation so they can be first to get their monies or whatever," Caroline said. "Maybe we could hide the serum someplace."

"They'd make you tell. I can do better than that," Fargo said. "How many syringes do you have?"

"I brought four," Caroline said.

"I'll take them," he said and waited as she fished the four syringes from a bag and handed them to him. "I'll ride out tonight and take these along. No needles, no inoculation. It'll be out of your hands."

"And tomorrow?"

"You can all follow the wagon tracks, just as you'd do anyway. I'll be plenty far ahead by then," Fargo said.

"Good luck," Ben said as he climbed out of the wagon. Caroline leaned forward, hands pressed against Fargo's chest.

"Find them, find them well enough to take the serum. That's the prayer I send with you," she said. He searched the pale-fire eyes, saw her struggle to find confidence, and saw that she could find only hope. He left, took the Ovaro into a clump of red cedar, and stretched out. The camp had already grown still, he saw. They'd sleep deep into the night, perhaps near dawn, before they woke. They'd retrieve their guns, then force Caroline to inoculate them. He let a grim smile touch his lips as he thought of their fury and their frustration. He closed his eyes, allowing himself an hour's sleep before he rose and walked the horse from the cedars.

He held the pinto to slow, careful steps and swung into the saddle only when he was some hundred yards from the wagons. Sending the horse into a trot, he rode north under the moon, finally halting before the moon reached the midnight sky. He let the horse roam as he stretched out on a bed of star moss in a stand of Utah juniper that stretched behind and ahead of him. He'd catnap, he decided, an hour or so at a time and rest in between. That would give him enough sleep and still make time when the cool of the night made riding easier. He closed his eyes and let his hearing tell him what the night whispered.

The soft scrape came to him and repeated itself. Too strong for a raccoon, claws too long for a weasel, movement too slow for a ferret. Badger, he decided, and listened to the distant howl of timber wolves. The short, careful steps of deer intruded and he caught the soft swish of brown bats as they swooped through the night. Nothing gave him pause for alarm and he had just closed his eyes when he caught the other sound, the rustle of sagebrush, then the drier sound of low brush being pressed down. He listened, eyes open to slits that let him see the figure moving toward him through the clump of juniper. He waited, one hand on the Colt lying at his side and watching the figure come closer and take shape under the moonlight. "I'll be damned," he said, sitting up as Holly halted. She wore a dark shirt and dark skirt over her compact figure.

"Followed you when you left the wagons. I thought you'd take off," she said. "It was hard. Thank God for a good moon."

"What do you think this is going to get you?" Fargo asked, standing up as she came still closer.

"What I want," she said. "Take me with you. I want the money Lila's got. It's not hers, it's ours."

"You want to risk catching the plague? That's being a fool," Fargo said.

"You're inoculated. You can get the money and give it to me," Holly said, her hand rising to the dark shirt. Her fingers worked at the buttons, and the shirt came open. She stood with her full, round breasts offering themselves boldly, each circled with a dark red areola and firm little tip. "Yours, anytime you want it, forever and ever. Randi and Terry, too. That's a promise," she murmured, keeping the skirt on as she waited. "You could start right now, if you like."

"Sorry," he said, not without a touch of rue in his voice.

"Come on, Fargo, you won't get another offer like this," Holly said.

"It's not the offer, it's the earning of it," he said, and her brow crinkled. "I'm here for saving, not collecting, for giving, not taking back. You'll have to wait your turn, if there is one."

Her round, full breasts lifted beautifully as she drew in a deep breath. She was certainly straining his self-discipline, he acknowledged inwardly. "You took the syringes," she said flatly.

He knew she caught the surprise that touched his face

113

before he could hold it back. "You're letting suspicion run away with you," he tried.

"Logic, not suspicion," Holly returned. "You left Caroline. You'd only do that if she was no good to us. That meant you took the syringes with you." He allowed a wry smile as he realized he had underestimated Holly's cleverness as well as her tenaciousness. "Give me the syringes," she said.

He returned a chiding half smile. "Button up and go back," he said, starting to walk from her.

"Not so fast," Holly said and he paused, glancing back at her to see her reach into her skirt and pull out the tiny pistol. A four-barreled Sharps derringer with silver trim around the edges, deadly and accurate at close range, its four barrels discharging in sequence.

"The working girl's best friend?" he commented.

"Sometimes," she said. "Like now. Put your gun on the ground, real slow, now. I wouldn't want our relationship to end badly."

"I wouldn't call this ending it well," Fargo said. The derringer didn't waver.

"Just a temporary disagreement," Holly said almost airily. "When I get the money I might hire you to see that we get back safely. So let's not do anything foolish. Just put the gun down."

He shrugged, lifted the Colt from its holster, and dropped it on the ground. "Now turn around," Holly said, and his lips were a thin line as he turned his back to her.

He heard her bend down and scoop up the Colt. She'd use it, of course, the derringer was not nearly heavy enough. He braced himself as he reached back into his thoughts, pulling upon old lessons and old tricks. He couldn't avoid the blow but maybe he could diminish the full force of it. It would be a matter of split second, instantaneous timing. A fraction of a second too late and the blow would hit him full force, a fraction of a second too soon and she'd realize what he was doing. The timing had to be perfect and that depended on his ears translating sound into a mental picture so precise he could follow her slightest movement. He closed his eyes and let his concentration shut out all else. He heard her turning the Colt in her hand, the sound of flesh against metal, then her foot pressed down dry buffalo grass as she took a single step forward. The soft sound of fabric against fabric told him she was raising her arm. When she brought the butt of the Colt down he felt the faint swish of air against the back of his neck.

He let his knees buckle just as the blow landed. It struck with force, enough force for him to feel the sharp stab of pain as he crumpled to the ground. He felt the dizziness sweep over him but he wasn't plunged into unconsciousness. He had timed it perfectly and as he lay with his eyes closed he heard her step past him. He opened his eyes just enough to peer out and see her beside the Ovaro, pulling his saddlebag open. He waited until she pushed the Colt into the waist of her skirt so she could use both hands to go through the saddlebag. Fighting off the pain that still shot through his head, he pushed to his feet. But not silently enough, he realized as Holly spun, saw him, and reached for the Colt. He flung himself forward in a low dive and caught her around the knees just as she got the gun out. She went backward as the horse skittered away and he landed atop her. He grabbed her wrist and twisted. The gun fell from her fingers and he twisted his thigh to take the blow as she tried to knee him in the groin.

Closing a hand around her arm, he spun her away,

then yanked her to her feet with him. "That's enough, dammit," he said harshly, and she glowered at him. He reached into her skirt pocket and removed the derringer.

"Bastard," she hissed.

"It's too late for flattery," he said, pulling her to the Ovaro. He took the lariat and dragged her to a young juniper.

"What are you doing?" She frowned, alarm coming into her voice.

"To quote you, you wouldn't want our relationship to end badly, would you?" he said. "I'm seeing that it doesn't. And keeping you out of my way."

"No, you can't," Holly protested as he began to tie her to the juniper. "You wouldn't leave me here alone."

"I can and I would," he said, tightening the lariat around her. "There's not too much left of the night. You'll be fine until the others find you. I expect they'll arrive sometime before noon. You'll be an unexpected surprise," he said.

"Goddamn you, Fargo, don't do this," Holly swore. She tried to twist herself free and found it was impossible. He swung onto the Ovaro as the moon moved toward the horizon line. "You son of a bitch," Holly screamed. "Rotten bastard."

"Don't say anything you'll be sorry for," he tossed at her as he sent the horse into a trot.

"I take back the offer," she shouted after him.

7

He kept a steady pace as he again followed the contours of the land, banking on the probability that the Turner wagons would stay to the easiest terrain. When the moon sank below the horizon line to plunge the land into stygian blackness, he halted and catnapped under a cluster of black maple until the new day broke. Climbing into the saddle again, he followed the wheel marks in the early light, and saw that they ran in an almost straight line north. The frown came to his brow as the tracks suddenly turned a sharp right and cut across the plain, and as he followed, he scanned the ground for pony prints. But he found none and continued to follow the tracks until he slowed as something rose on the land directly ahead.

Putting the horse into a walk, he moved forward as the mound began to take shape, such as it was. When he reined to a halt the bitter oath welled up inside him and he stared at the terrible scene. The blackened, charred remains of the wagons held him first. Some were marked only by a few pieces of iron drive shafts and twisted metal braces. In one he saw the brass frame of a bed still standing, a strangely grotesque monument to a disaster. What he saw and what he didn't see told him the terrible truth of what had happened. No Indian attack, this, the wagons placed neatly side by side. The horses had been unhitched to go their way and none had stayed around, he noted. He searched the scene with his eyes, pausing at each burned and blackened object, some with only a few bones still remaining, others reduced to charred cinders among the equally charred remains of the wagons. A few shreds of cloth that had somehow survived still clung to a blackened piece of wood, and a dozen iron pots and pans were scattered throughout the grisly scene.

But one wagon had been placed a half-dozen feet beyond the others and amid its burnt remains, what was left of a figure leaned against half a wheel that somehow still stood upright. As he drew a deep breath and continued to scan the scene, an object some ten yards from the burned-out center caught his eye. He dismounted and walked to where a flat, leather pouch had been placed and held down with three rocks. Squatting on his haunches, he pushed aside the rocks, picked up the pouch, and drew out three sheets of paper from inside, each covered with neat, careful handwriting. Even before he began to read aloud, he knew he held the record of the last events of a terrible, tragic story.

Dear Caroline,

I hope you will eventually come upon these words. Perhaps even before you do, you will have suspected that you would be too late. But you will not give way to that suspicion. I know you. But do not berate yourself. I know you tried. Unfortunately, the plague has spread, refused to allow any of us to avoid its fatal touch. Perhaps you came across the graves of the Osgoods and the Torrances. The people here, whatever their faults, have acted bravely.

They have cared for each other, helped each other, tended to the dead and the dying. Perhaps being all touched by the same terrible fate gives us all a new way of looking at each other. But now the final time has come. There are but a few of us still able to drive. Most of us are already dead. We are wagons tied together carrying the lifeless, pulled by horses who seem to sense the need for good behavior. Because smallpox is such a highly contagious plague, when the last of us dies we will still pose a terrible threat to anyone coming upon us.

The lifeless and all of our belongings will carry the infection and we will transmit it to any good samaritan or hapless Indian who comes by to see to our wagons. I cannot allow this to happen. I cannot allow us to infect the innocent with this deadly pox. The only way to prevent this is, as I'm sure you realize, to burn ourselves and our belongings. The consuming power of fire is the only gift we have to give or else risk spreading the plague even further to the innocent and unaware.

I have decided this is our only decent course. As it is becoming plain that I will be the last to go, I have decided to set down here what I shall do. It will be a final record of the last hours of the Turner wagon train. My last act will be to set the wagons afire, but I must arrange to make my own the last one. Martyrdom, I am learning, takes a special kind of courage or faith. Possessing neither that kind of courage nor faith, I know I could not stoicly let fire consume me. I am too weak for that. I would flee at the last moment, run, and continue to be a source of infection, perhaps lying unconscious somewhere, to whoever came along.

I cannot do that. Everyone and everything here must perish with the cleansing power of fire. Therefore, I shall take the revolver Frank Turner has given me and tie myself to the wagon wheel. I will make so many knots that I will have no chance to undo them before the flames reach me. I will set the wagon afire and when the moment comes, use the gun on myself. The flames will do the rest. They will consume everything with it and wipe out the plague that is upon us so we can contaminate no one else. It is the right thing to do. Besides, my dear Caroline, it is no great sacrifice as death is but hours away in any case. We are merely robbing death of its power to lie in wait.

I know you have tried to reach us and bless you for that, Caroline. Attached are some messages written by a few before they died. I'm sure they will mean something to somebody. Good-bye to you all.

Set down this first day of June, 1860,

Dr. Harvey Dodson

Fargo glanced at the pieces of paper attached to the letter and let a wry sound escape his lips. Returning everything to the flat leather pouch, he rose, walked a dozen feet away, and seated himself on the dry buffalo grass. His eyes swept the charred and blackened bits and pieces of what had once been a wagon train, what had once been human beings filled with plans and dreams, hopes and fears. But everything, the good and the bad, had been destroyed by events beyond their control. Somehow, it seemed worse than had they been slaughtered by an Arapaho attack. It was so impersonal, everything wiped out by an enemy you could neither see, nor hear, nor smell nor touch, an enemy that robbed one of the dignity of defending oneself.

He felt terribly sorry for the dead and terribly helpless at not having reached them in time, but also terribly small. He thought about the power of forces beyond man's control and of what some would call the inevitability of fate. He accepted the first but rebelled against the second. Fate, he pondered, too often got credit it didn't deserve. It was more often dictated by the actions of men and women and blamed on the mysterious force of fate. His jaw tightened as he thought back to a man named Mexico Jack. His vicious cupidity had cost precious days that might have gotten the serum to the wagons in time. Not fate at all but human greed. He was still contemplating the forces of life and death when he saw the wagons appear, rolling toward him, Caroline first, then the big Percherons following.

He rose as they rolled to a halt, their eyes staring at the charred scene and it was Caroline who spoke first, her voice catching as she did. "Is this . . . is this . . . ?" she began.

"Yes," he said and pulled the letter from the pouch and handed it to her. "Read it to the others," he said and stood back. They listened in silence and when she finished, Harry Adamson was the first to rush forward into the area where the charred residue of the wagons covered the ground.

"Gone, all the money gone," he croaked. "Nothing left . . . nothing. All burned up."

Holly, Terry, and Randi took a step forward as they stared at the scene. "Goddamn her," Holly breathed. "Goddamn the bitch."

Fargo watched Herb Baxter wander through the scene, aimlessly staring at the blackened remains of one wagon after another, pausing at the pieces of human remains still visible. "I can't tell anyone," he murmured. "I can't recognize anyone, anything."

"Does it matter?" Fargo said. "Nobody got away. Everyone's there. No winners, no survivors. Fire wrote the final chapter for all of them. You, too." Herb Baxter looked at him through eyes dulled with shock, the totality of it still penetrating him. Fargo took the last sheet of paper from the pouch. "There are a few messages here," he said, pausing.

"Go on, read them," Holly said.

"This first one's from Lila Tomkins. If you girls are still chasing me, you lose," Fargo read.

"Bitch. Goddamn bitch," Holly hissed.

Fargo turned to Adamson. "There's one here from Donald Burton," he said.

"Go on." Adamson growled.

"To Harry," Fargo read. "Shakespeare wrote that the evil that men do lives after them. He was right."

"That doesn't do me much good. The money's gone," Adamson said.

"It didn't do him much good, either," Fargo said.

"All for nothing," Ernie Alden said. "It's over and it was for nothing."

"Except it's not over," Fargo said as he heard the sound of hoofbeats and turned to see the riders appear, some ten of them. He saw Shepley Reisner's thick-lipped, self-indulgent face leading the others as they came to a halt, the man surveying the scene with a dark frown pushing across his brow.

"What the hell is this?" Reisner growled.

"This is what's left of the Turner wagons," Fargo said, glancing at Caroline and seeing the tension come into her face. He stepped to her and she saw the warning in his eyes.

"Who are you?" Shepley Reisner asked.

"We've been following the Turner train, trying to catch up to them," Fargo said, his eyes flicking to the other men with Reisner. Gunslingers, his quick glance told him, hard-eyed men with cold faces, men who enjoyed killing. His gaze went back to Shepley Reisner, and he saw the man frowning at Caroline.

"You were the one to bring serum to them, right?" Reisner asked, and Caroline nodded. The man's frown stayed. "I heard your serum was stolen," he said.

"How'd you hear that?" Caroline challenged.

"Word gets around," Reisner answered. "How come you're still following them?" he asked, suspicion coloring his tone.

"We wanted to help if we could, serum or no serum," Fargo answered. "These folks all had friends in those wagons." He waited as Reisner turned the answer over in his mind. "It seemed the decent thing to do," Fargo added.

"Guess so," Reisner said after another moment. "Seems you're too late," he said, sweeping the scene again with disappointment in his face. One of his men broke into his frowning thoughts.

"That wagon train we saw south of here, bet they'd like to know about this," the man said. "I'd say it was our duty to tell them."

"Yes, you're right," Shepley Reisner said, wheeling his horse in a tight circle. "There's nothing to do for us here. Let's ride." He sent his horse into a fast canter and the others charged after him as Fargo waited till they rode from sight.

"We get away with it?" Ben asked.

"I'm not betting on it. I don't think he was really satisfied with our answer. Somewhere along the way he's going to stop and take a look at those serum boxes they're carrying."

"Maybe not until they reach that wagon train," Caroline said.

"Wouldn't count on it," Fargo said. "We're going to ride and ride as fast as we can." As the others climbed onto wagons and horses, he let his eyes linger a moment longer at the blackened scene of death and despair. The secrets and answers that remained would stay that way forever. Whoever had arranged for the original attack on Caroline's wagon would be forever shrouded in silence. It didn't much matter any longer, he realized. Retribution had come in its own way. Pulling his eyes from the scene, he led the way northwest across the sagebrush-dotted plain. Behind him the wagons creaked and jounced as they raced all out after him. He had ridden some fifteen minutes when he glanced back to see Caroline on one of the extra horses. She was riding to catch up to him and he slowed.

"Thought I'd ride along with you," she said.

"Don't expect conversation," he said.

"You're worried," she said.

"That's for damn sure," he said.

"It's gone badly. I guess omens don't always work out," Caroline said.

"Bull's-eye," he said grimly as the open land grew less open with large clusters of the black maple crowding the land. The trees became plentiful enough to slow the following wagons but not thick enough to provide a hiding place and he cursed softly. He'd wracked his brain as he rode and had come up with no way to avoid the inevitable. He was reduced to searching for some spot to try and make a stand and not getting far with that. More clusters of black maple crowded the open passages and when a small stream cut in front of him he dismounted to let the horses drink. Caroline came to stand beside him and he saw the dejection in her face.

"Still thinking about how it ended?" he asked.

"Yes," she murmured, somehow able to fill the single word with infinite pain. "I failed, completely."

"Stop beating on yourself. You tried. You can't do more than that," Fargo offered.

"Others followed me," she said.

"For their own reasons, most of them selfish. Their choice," he said.

She slid her arms around his neck. "Not you, or old Ben," she said, and he felt the soft warmth of her lips. "You've been wonderful. You trusted in me and I let you down," she said.

"I've made worse guesses," he said. "Let's get riding."

"You still think we've a chance?" she asked and he heard the hope in her voice.

"There's bad luck and there's good luck. We've had the first. Maybe we can make the second," he said.

"Make the second?" She frowned.

"That's right. Luck doesn't usually come up and shout at you, leastwise not good luck. It hides, waits for you to recognize it, then make what you can out of it," he said and she was silent as she turned his words over in her mind. The trees thinned a little but as he rode on he felt the Ovaro's gait change. Slowing, he again felt the horse change gait and he halted beside a cluster of black maple and leaned to one side as he stared at the ground. The furrow spread across his brow as he dismounted and Caroline came alongside him. The furrow became a frown as he stared at the ground. It moved, slid sideways, bulged upward, shifted, rose, and suddenly it wasn't just soil and grass shoots but a carpet of shiny carapaces, transparent wings, and tiny legs, all moving, wriggling, pushing, an emerging, escaping swarm of tens of thousands of crawling insects.

"My God." Caroline gasped. "What are they?"

"Locusts," Fargo said.

"Seventeen-year locusts?" Caroline queried.

"Twenty, seventeen, fourteen, ten, four, take your pick. There are damn near a hundred species that take different periods to lay dormant and finally emerge. But they all have one thing in common. When they emerge, they emerge all at once," he said as the two wagons appeared and rolled to a halt. Fargo ran a finger along the nearest tree branch and then went to a half dozen more and pointed to long marks that ran along the sides of the branches. "See these slits?" he asked.

"Yes," Caroline answered as she followed the path of his fingers across the narrow marks.

"They're egg scars. The female locust cuts slits in young branches and deposits eggs in them. When the eggs hatch, the young locusts, without wings, drop to the ground, where they burrow in anywhere from four to twenty years, depending on the species. It's been going on the same way since the world began."

"The Bible speaks about plagues of locusts," Ben Smith put in.

"That's right. When they emerge, tens of thousands of them, they swarm over everything and anything, eating, sucking, crushing, suffocating by their sheer numbers, overwhelming whatever's in their path," Fargo said, and he saw Caroline staring at the ground with a mixture of fear and disgust.

"There are more of them pushing up," she said.

"They're emerging, getting ready to erupt in flight. They'll explode as one, a swarm so dense they'll blot out the sun," Fargo said.

"Christ, let's get out of here," Ernie Alden said.

"Wait, not so fast," Fargo said, his eyes narrowed at the soil underfoot. "Maybe we just got a reprieve."

"What are you talking about?" Holly frowned.

"I'm talking about one plague for another," Fargo said. "We were too late for one plague. Maybe another can save us."

"Save us from Reisner?" Ben asked.

"That's right. He's on his way. I'm sure of it and we won't have a chance. But maybe we will, now," Fargo said.

"Because of the locusts?" Caroline questioned.

"That's right. They'll give us a chance, but we'll have to be real lucky. They'll have to emerge at just the right time, the thousands on thousands of them. If that happens, maybe we stay alive," Fargo said. He scanned the ground again, soil that now moved on its own, sliding and pushing, becoming alive with a swarming mass of tiny bodies. They were almost ready to become a plague of inundating, consuming, suffocating creatures, nature's latest incarnation of the Good Book's "plague of locusts." But could they change a plague into a blessing, suffocation into salvation? He grimaced at the question even as he knew he had to try. "Follow me," he ordered the others. "Very slowly. We don't want to set them off. They're damn close to it now."

Keeping the Ovaro at a slow walk, he moved the horse forward and heard the sound of clicking mandibles and rubbing wings begin to increase. Yet he didn't dare move faster, the seething, stirring mass of insects poised to erupt. He felt the perspiration coating his face and he glanced back and saw each face tight with tension. All except Caroline. She seemed simply drained by all that had happened, failure and defeat taking the fire from her and leaving only paleness. She had brought caring and compassion with her and seen it all swept away. She, of them all, deserved better, he thought, straining his eyes as he peered into the distance.

Suddenly he felt the edge of excitement catch at him as he saw the earth begin to grow still another hundred yards ahead. The locusts had come to the end of their long dormant breeding grounds and he fought away the urge to break into a trot. Slowly, the shifting, seething soil began to grow still and he led the wagons on another hundred yards before he motioned them to a halt. "Line the wagons up and unhitch the horses," he said and drew a question from Holly.

"They'll take off," she said.

"That's the idea. Most of the locusts will form one huge swarm but some always spread out. They could come this way, too. The horses will get away on their own. We can round them up later," Fargo explained and waited as the horses were quickly unhitched. He stepped to the wagons as the others turned to him. "Wrap your heads. Leave only room to see. When you're finished, find a spot beneath or inside the wagons. Keep your guns covered until you're ready to fire them. I've heard of swarms of locusts jamming the firing mechanisms." He tied the Ovaro's reins around the horse's neck and sent the horse trotting off by itself toward the big Percherons idly nibbling at buffalo grass. Wrapping his kerchief around his face, Fargo crawled beneath the wagon where Caroline lay, only her eyes visible behind the veils of cloth she had wrapped around herself. Ben

Smith lay on his stomach beside her, hat pulled low and kerchief covering his face.

Fargo's eyes peered across the land. A flicker of insects rose up and settled back down again and then, in the distance, the knot of horsemen appeared. "Here they come," he called out, his voice muffled behind the kerchief. "They found out they've been carrying rocks."

"What if the locusts don't swarm?" Harry Adamson asked.

"We're in big trouble," Fargo said.

"I say give them the goddamn serum. That's what they want," Adamson said.

"You think that'll keep you alive?" Fargo said. "You think they'll say thank you and good-bye?" Adamson fell silent and Fargo's eyes swept the scene from beneath the wagon. "Come on. Take off, you little bastards. You've had a long enough sleep, dammit. Come on," he urged. Reisner and his men thundered toward them. If they were aware of the locusts they didn't comprehend the immediacy of what was waiting to happen, all their attention on the two wagons. Fargo brought the big Henry up to his shoulder as it seemed that his gamble on nature's cycle had failed. Irony filled the bitter sound that escaped his lips. This would be a first, he told himself. He had been in trouble because men had failed to do their part. This would be the first time locusts had put him behind the eight ball.

Though his eyes were glued to the scene unfolding in front of him, it still happened with an awesome explosion of motion. Tens of thousands of wings and bodies exploded upward as one, taking wing simultaneously. In seconds, the very air was a dark mass, a swarming, blanketing, winged wall, impossible to see through, around, or above. It grew, thickened, and rose and he felt the sudden deluge of creatures settling on the wagons, working their way into every crevice. But it was only the fringe of the main swarm, he realized, and he shouted through his kerchief to the others. "Stay in place. Don't panic," he called, shooting a glance at Caroline and seeing her shrouded figure settle down. The swarming insects continued to fill the air and Fargo watched the dense mass begin to move, a ponderous motion overwhelming everything in its path.

Somewhere in the center of it, Shepley Reisner and his men were trying to fight their way out of the suffocating density that had descended on them. Their horses, also fighting to get away from the winged hordes, would already have thrown some. Others were hunched over, eyes closed, trying to urge their horses to run. But the attack was consuming, Fargo knew, a relentless assault that brought the ancient Scriptures to life again. Fargo's eyes caught a movement at the base of the swarm and he saw two horses racing out of the cloud of locusts, riderless and kicking their fore and hind legs into the air as they ran in an effort to dislodge the insects that still clung to them. He watched another riderless horse race into the clear, and then from the left, two riders clinging to their saddles emerged on their horses. They raced on and Fargo brought the big Henry up. Caroline turned to glance at him.

"They get away, they'll come back for us," Fargo said, tightened his finger on the trigger and watched the first rider topple from his horse, then the second. Two more riderless horses ran from the swarm, then a horse with a rider flattened on his saddle. Fargo fired again and the figure fell to the ground. His gaze went back to the swarm, saw it moving south, a skyborne curtain of locusts that still blotted out the sky. Three more riderless horses managed to gallop into the clear and then a lone figure, half stumbling, half tottering, bloodied hands clutched to his face. The big Henry barked again and the figure fell facedown and lay still. "Call that a mercy killing," Fargo muttered. He stayed in place as the locusts that had descended on the wagons began to take wing, small bunches breaking away to rejoin the main swarm. Two more horses came from the black maple and ran off together, still followed by small knots of the insects.

His eyes went back to the main swarm, saw that they hadn't changed their inexorable, slow movement south, encompassing, overwhelming everything in their path, and he crawled from beneath the wagon, pushed to his feet, and drew the kerchief from his face. Pushing his hat back, he waited for the others to come from the wagons and unwrap themselves. They fell in behind him as he started to walk across the ground, where the thousands upon thousands of locusts had emerged. The bodies came into sight, curled on the ground, many in fetal positions as they attempted to protect themselves. His jaw grew tight as he saw the hordes of insects that had smothered every part, pore, and opening of the lifeless figures. They clogged nostrils, eyes, and ears, crawled through hair, and spilled out of mouths that hung open and disgorged their bodies.

Behind him, he heard Holly gag, and he had to force himself to peer at the scene, count bodies, and search for life he knew he'd not find. He thought he recognized the swollen, misshapen face of Shepley Reisner under the hundreds of insects still blanketing the figure. But he couldn't be sure of the suffocated figure and he went on until he was reasonably certain no one had escaped. He turned and walked back to the wagons as the others followed. "Plagues of locusts," Ben Smith muttered. "Not just words out of the Bible but here and now."

"We were lucky. It all came together for us," Fargo said.

"What was it you said about making your luck?" Caroline reminded him. "You recognized it and made the luck work."

"Start walking. We've horses to round up," Fargo said and began to stride north. He found the Ovaro as the horse heard his whistle and came. In the saddle, he rode out, finally spotting the Percherons and herding them to where the others had crisscrossed the field. It took time but the other horses were finally rounded up and returned to the wagons. He led the way for another half hour. Dusk had begun to slide over the land when he found a place to bed down, near a stand of Utah juniper.

They ate quickly and it was Caroline who broke the silence when the meal was over. "I don't know what the rest of you plan to do but Ben and I are going back to Green Springs with the serum. I hope we won't have to use it there but we'll have it if we do," she said and turned to Fargo. "I'm hoping you'll take us back."

"Part of the way," he said, and Caroline frowned.

"Made a promise. I intend to keep it," he said and her frown stayed as she peered at him.

"The girl at the way station?" she said and he heard the disapproval come into her voice.

"Melita." He nodded. "Without her, you wouldn't have the serum. You'd never have gotten it back. She told me where Mexico Jack had gone. I promised to come back and take her from him."

Caroline's lips pursed as she said nothing and climbed

into her wagon while the others turned away. Fargo settled some twenty-five yards from the wagons under a low-branched tree. After taking off his shirt, he stretched out on the bedroll. He lay awake, listening to the night, when he heard someone approach. He rose on one elbow to see Caroline. She dropped to her knees at the edge of the bedroll, a loose nightdress cloaking her pale beauty. "You decided the hell with what anyone else thinks?" he asked.

"In a way. I want to stay here with you," she said. "But I keep wondering."

"About what?" he asked.

"If keeping a promise is the only reason you're going back for her," Caroline said, and he didn't hide the surprise in his face. "I saw the way she looked at you. You did, too. It had to do with invitations, not promises," Caroline said.

"Maybe it did but that doesn't change anything. She kept her part of it. I'm keeping mine. It's as simple as that," he said.

"Nothing's simple between men and women," she said.

"I'll go along with that," he agreed. "I didn't figure you for the possessive type."

"I didn't, either. That's your fault. You make a woman possessive," she said almost crossly.

"Get some sleep. This'll keep for another time," he said and she stretched out on the bedroll beside him. It was only minutes when he heard her steady breathing as she slept. He closed his eyes. She felt nice beside him and he was aware of the tension of the day still clinging. He welcomed slumber, let it come to him quickly and deeply. Plunged into the depths of new sleep, he lay deep in the cocoon of the night as the hours drifted on.

The soft sound woke him, and he thought it was Caroline turning. Until he felt the hard, cold pressure against his neck. He knew what it was before he opened his eyes and cursed under his breath.

8

Thoughts tumbled through his mind as he pulled his eyes open. But not the usual thoughts. Not surprise, not rage, not fear, not frustration. An overwhelming disappointment swept through him, a profound disappointment in human beings, deeper than he had ever felt before. "Don't do anything dumb," Harry Adamson's voice said, and the pistol pressed harder into his neck and Fargo's lips pulled back.

He turned slowly. Randi and Terry were pulling Caroline to her feet, and Randi was holding a rifle to her ribs. Fargo stared at Harry Adamson. "Why? After everything that's happened?" he asked, not ashamed of the incredulity that seized him. "You could have been dead, three times over, but you're not. You're alive. Doesn't that mean anything to you? Don't any of you have any sense of thankfulness?"

"You're alive thanks to Fargo," Caroline put in.

"You ought to be counting your blessings," Fargo said.

"Counting our blessings won't get us any money," Randi answered and glancing at her, Fargo saw the movement that became Holly's sturdy figure. She stayed back, looking on.

"Is that all that counts? Money?" Fargo questioned.

"I'm getting something out of all this. That bastard stole a lot of money from me. I want to make up for some of it," Adamson said.

"Money you both stole from somebody else," Fargo mentioned.

"Shut up," Adamson rasped and Fargo saw the wildness in his eyes. "The damn serum will bring a good price. We'll do what Reisner was going to do, sell it and split what we get."

"Blood money, for real," Caroline said.

"You shut up, too," Randi shouted at her.

"Where's Ernie Alden?" Fargo asked.

"He left and rode off on his own. He said he wanted to get back to Washington and see about getting control of his patent. He didn't care about the money," Adamson said. "That's fine with us."

"Ben Smith?" Caroline queried.

"Out cold in the wagon. We didn't want any problems with him," Adamson said. He stepped back but Fargo eyed the gun. The man held it steady and aimed it at his chest. Fargo shifted, but didn't push to his feet. He let himself rise onto one knee, his right leg away from Adamson. His glance went to Randi, who held the rifle poked into Caroline's ribs. Terry stood alongside her and Holly still stayed in the background. He let his eyes hold on Randi for a moment, studying her face. Then he glanced at Terry, and finally at Adamson again. Their faces held the same note, wild desperation. They had only one thing left inside them, pure greed, and that meant they had crossed the line that separated the rational from the irrational, the sane from the insane.

They were beyond caring and beyond reaching, prepared to kill because they had rejected any other course, passed any other choice. The consuming power of greed dictated their every thought, their every act, and he swore silently as he was aware that they had dictated his own course. They had given him no choice. He had to act with their unfeeling, uncaring ruthlessness or lose forever. His hand crept upward along his right leg and slid the edge of his jeans upward as he stayed on one knee, his eyes on Adamson. "Let's get rid of them both together," Randi said, and the man nodded.

"Get up," he ordered Fargo and took a step closer. Fargo's fingers were around the hilt of the double-edged blade in the calf holster, his body still blocking Adamson's view. The blade came into his hand as he slowly started to rise and he was almost upright when his arm flashed upward in a lightninglike, upward swipe. The blade sliced into Adamson's wrist and the man let out a curse of pain as the gun fell from his hand. But Fargo was already following through, his arm striking out in a flat arc. Adamson's head fell forward as a torrent of red rushed from his neck.

"Goddamn," Randi cursed. She swung the rifle and fired. Fargo felt Adamson's body shudder with the two shots that plowed into it as Fargo held it upright as a shield. But Adamson was already dead, and as he crumpled to the ground Fargo's arm came up in a short arc. The thin throwing knife whistled through the air in an upward trajectory. Randi saw it only as it slammed into the cleavage between her breasts, imbedding itself to the hilt. Her mouth fell open but there was no sound from her. Her eyes held a terrible realization.

She staggered forward two steps to topple facedown as the rifle fell from her hands. As she lay still, Fargo heard the scream of fury split the air and looked up to see Terry charging for the rifle. He leaped, reaching her just as she scooped up the gun. He kicked, hitting the rifle just as she brought it up to fire. The gun flew upward just as her finger tightened on the trigger, and Fargo saw her fall backward. Her body jerked spasmodically as the bullet traveled upward through her until she collapsed with a final spasm. Fargo saw Caroline on the ground, where she had flung herself, and his eyes rose to find Holly, still standing to one side. He watched her hands as he moved in a half-crouch toward her. "Where's the derringer," he rasped.

"No more bullets for it," Holly said. He halted in front of her, his eyes cold as ice floes as they bored into her. "It was Randi's idea. Terry and Adamson went along with it," Holly said.

"No way. Randi never had an idea in her life. This was your play," Fargo said.

"I stayed back. You saw me," Holly protested.

"Yes, you're the smart one. You know me by now. You knew it mightn't go right. You stayed back, played both sides of the street," Fargo said. "But it was your call."

Her eyes narrowed at him. "You don't know that," she said, the answer its own admission.

"We both know it," Fargo said. "Take one of the extra horses and start riding."

"You going to leave me alone out here?" Holly protested.

"It's more than you planned for us," he said as he saw the first pink of dawn touch the sky. "Take it before I change my mind," Fargo said with a growl. Holly studied his face with sullen anger and decided he was not a man of idle threats.

"Bastard," she hissed as she strode to her wagon in the light of the new day. Stuffing things into two pouches, she took one of the extra horses and cast a narrow-eyed glare at him as she prepared to ride away. "You're really stupid. You could've had a sweet deal. You'll be sorry," she threatened. He watched her put the horse into a fast trot and become a small figure receding across the plain.

"I'm sorry already," he muttered, staring after her as Caroline came to stand beside him.

"Forget about her. You did the right thing," Caroline said.

"Why don't I feel better?" he asked.

"You're naturally suspicious," she said. "Let's see to Ben and get away from here." Fargo followed her to the wagon, where with cold water from a canteen she brought the old man around and put a poultice on the swelling on his temple. When he felt able to drive, they set out, the Percherons and the other wagon tied behind on a long tether. Fargo stayed in tree cover and narrow passages wherever possible, now that cover was more important than time. The day was finally drawing to a close when he found a stand of thick-branched cottonwoods.

"You can bed down here," he said as he dismounted and let the Ovaro drink from a bucket hanging on the converted hay wagon. Caroline paused beside him, her eyes on the Ovaro.

"You still have the saddle on him," she observed, and he didn't say anything. "You're not staying," she said. "You're going to the way station."

"There's a cut over the hills that'll save me a lot of time," he said. "You go on come morning. Stay in tree cover as I've done. Keep south till you reach the Sunrise River. Follow it east until it curves north. Leave it then and go southeast. You'll come on to Green Springs in a few days."

Her arms slid around his neck. "I don't want you to go," she said.

"For the wrong reasons." He smiled.

"I won't deny that. I don't want her being grateful with you. But I don't want anything to happen to you. I want more than the memory of one night. How's that for honesty?" she said.

"Pretty damn good," he said.

"You can't keep every promise," Caroline said.

"You're right. Lots of things make that impossible. But it's not the keeping that counts. It's the trying," he said. She searched his face and was silent and he knew she understood, perhaps unhappily, yet she understood. Her lips touched his as dark descended, a brief, soft moment, and then she stepped back and walked away. He climbed onto the Ovaro and waved at Ben Smith as he rode from beneath the trees.

The moon rose as he made his way across a series of low hills until he halted under a midnight sky and slept in between a pair of Rocky Mountain maples. When morning came, he rode on through the hills, searching for markers that hung in his mind and the day neared an end when the hills descended to an end. Before the night fell, he saw the land grow dry and the juniper grow plentiful and he knew he had only to ride forward. He kept a steady pace as the moon rose, weaving his way in and out amid the stands of juniper, the terrain fashioned of familiar markers.

The moon had climbed close to the midnight sky when he slowed. He drew to a halt and slid from the horse. The sprawling, flat-roofed buildings of the way station took shape in front of him, their drab ugliness softened by the moonlight. He moved closer on foot, the Ovaro following, then he circled to the side of the buildings and tethered the horse to a low branch in a cluster of junipers. Moving forward again in a crouch, he paused at the corral fence and scanned the main building of the inn, where a dim lamp glowed just inside the entranceway. His eyes went to the darkened windows, and slowly moving across the right wing of the building, he looked to the left, searching for a sign to tell him which was Melita's room. It seemed a fruitless search and he grimaced at the thought of going from room to room when suddenly his eyes came to a halt at the last window of the left wing of the inn.

A dress fluttered from the windowsill, hung there to dry. Fargo smiled grimly as he moved forward. He stayed in a crouch and paused at the doorway to the inn. He listened, heard only silence, and went into the building. Long, silent steps brought him to the last room of the long corridor and he closed one hand around the doorknob, slowly turned it, and felt the door open. He stepped into the room and paused, letting his eyes adjust to the darkness for a moment. He found the bed near the window. He discerned the figure covered by a sheet, and he stepped on the balls of his feet as he crossed the room. She lay facedown, the sheet over the back of her head. The last thing he wanted was a scream of surprise. He slowly reached down and brought his hand alongside the side of her face, sliding it over her mouth.

She woke instantly and he felt her stiffen. "Shhh . . . it's me, Fargo," he whispered. She stayed stiffened a moment and he felt her relax. Her head nodded under the sheet and he drew his hand back. She turned, a quick motion, flinging herself around and the sheet fell away from her face and he stared down at her. He felt his breath draw in with a sharp gasp of surprise. The face that looked back at him wasn't the olive-skinned, black-haired one he expected but a slightly pudgy, round face with reddish tinted hair. He also found himself staring at the muzzle of a big Remington single-action army revolver.

"Surprise," Holly said. "Get back." He eyed the revolver, and realizing that it could send bullets tearing through his stomach in split seconds he took a step backward. Holly swung her legs over the edge of the bed. She kicked hard and sent a tin pail filled with stones crashing into the wall, exploding the night with a loud din. Running footsteps followed in seconds and the door burst open as Mexico Jack and two other men rushed in, guns drawn. Mexico Jack halted, glanced at Fargo, and an oily smile spread across his face.

"Well, now, we have caught our fox," he said, and Fargo's eyes stayed on Holly as thoughts raced through his mind. She had been there when he told Caroline he was returning for Melita, had some six hours' start, and came here first. They'd just set up the trap for him then, waited, and he'd done the rest. He cursed silently and included himself.

"You've been a real son of a bitch pain in the ass," Holly said to him. "Without you we can get the serum, split what it'll bring."

"Miss Holly is a young woman of great determination," Mexico Jack said as one of the others lighted a lamp.

"She's a young woman of great stupidity," Fargo said, his eyes on Holly. Her eyes narrowed at him.

"I'm going to get my money out of this. You're getting a bullet. I know who's stupid," she said.

He uttered a harsh laugh. He wanted to find a way to reach her. "You really think this weasel is going to share anything with you?" Fargo asked and grunted in pain as

142

Mexico Jack's blow slammed into his temple. But he saw an instant of alarm touch Holly's eyes, let a moment of hope stir inside him.

"Take his gun," Mexico Jack ordered and one of the men yanked the Colt from its holster.

"He wears a damn knife around his leg," Holly said, and Fargo knew he had lost. She was past reaching. She had thrown her lot in with Mexico Jack. He represented her last chance, greed and desperation blinding her to anything else. And perhaps one more thing, he realized. Perhaps Holly and Mexico Jack were two of a kind, uncaring and ruthless. It would not be the first time the totally selfish had joined together for their own good. One of the men found the blade in the calf holster and pulled it free and handed it to Mexico Jack along with the Colt.

"Where's Melita?" Fargo asked.

"Bring him," Mexico Jack said and the two men poked their guns into his ribs from both sides and walked him from the room. Holly followed as he was led down the corridor, across the wide dining room with its wooden tables and Mexico Jack unlocked a door at the far side, yanked it open and Fargo felt himself pushed into a barren room. A figure stirred from the floor, a lamp burning low affording light and Fargo felt the wave of shock sweep over him. Nude, the figure half turned and Fargo stared at the bruised, battered, and bloodied body and face.

"My God," he said and dropped to one knee beside Melita. Through swollen eyes she forced to open, she looked at him and he couldn't tell if the swollen lips tried to smile. She made a sound and a trickle of blood came from her mouth and she bent over to rest facedown on the ground. He saw two jagged ends of rib bones protruding from her side and he rose, his fists clenched as he moved toward Mexico Jack. "You bastard. You rotten, stinking bastard," he rasped.

Mexico Jack pulled his six-gun out, as did the other two men. Fargo halted, the muscles in his neck throbbing. "I did not do that to her," he said.

"Who did?" Fargo growled.

"She betrayed me. I learn that when Miss Holly arrive. I beat her but she kick me and run away. She try to take a horse, run into the corral. She scares the horses. They kick, knock her down and stomp her," the man said, his tone matter-of-fact.

"And you just threw her in here?" Fargo said.

Mexico Jack shrugged. "She is dead. It just hasn't come to her yet."

"She was running from you. That makes it your fault in my book," Fargo said.

"I don't care about your book. You are dead, too," the man said, turning to Holly. "We kill him now? He can be dangerous, you said."

"But maybe he can be valuable. I've been thinking," Holly said. "I ought to get something out of him for all the trouble he's caused me. We'll take the serum but I think Caroline would pay good money to save his life. She is that kind."

Fargo heard in her voice the contempt she had for sincerity, for human decency, for honest caring. Mexico Jack's voice cut into his thoughts. "Good. Then we take him with us, an added prize," the man said.

"No. We leave him here and come back for him. He is too damn tricky. He'll find some way to do something," Holly said.

"Whatever you say." Mexico Jack shrugged and stepped to the door, Holly and the other two men following. He pulled the door closed after him and Fargo heard the lock being turned from the other side. Dropping down on one knee beside Melita, he gently touched her black hair. It seemed the only place that didn't carry a bruise, a welt, or torn flesh. "I will find a way out for us," he said.

She answered in a voice barely audible, her words voicing the terrible reality he didn't want to face. "There is no way out for me. Inside, I am gone, broken, everything broken." She paused, fighting for strength, and her voice came again, a hoarse whisper. "You can get out, save yourself," she said, pausing again to find the strength to go on. "There are old rags in the corner, put there a long time ago. There is a key under them. It unlocks the door from in here." She paused again, gathering her breath, and went on. "I put it there a long time ago. He used to lock me in here when he was mad at me. I wanted to be able to get out if I had to. Now it is yours to use."

She fell back onto her side and he heard the wheezing of her crushed lungs and smashed ribs. Gently, he stroked the black hair and cursed an oily, evil, ruthless predator. He didn't leave Holly out. Mexico Jack would never have known if she hadn't come here. Her story had triggered everything that had happened to Melita. She and her consuming greed shared the guilt. He rose, went to the corner, and pawed through the collection of old rags. The key appeared, at the very bottom, and he pushed it into his pocket. He'd wait. He wouldn't chance emerging into a hail of bullets. Dawn wasn't far away and he returned to Melita, lay down beside her, and rested his hand on her head.

"Hold on," he told her. "Don't give up."

Her head turned and he thought the battered lips formed a gentle smile. "It is all right, my good friend.

You have given me something to take with me," she said. "You came back for me. That is more than anyone has ever done for me." A shudder of a sigh wracked her body and she fell silent. He lay down beside her, one hand on her head, and he listened to the sounds of her tortured breathing and made another promise to Melita. "He'll pay. They both will," he murmured and held his hand on her head as the night moved on. He closed his eyes after a while, catnapped, and suddenly he woke, the total silence enveloping him. He pushed up on one elbow, bent down to the small form beside him, and swore softly when he rose. He gathered the rags from the corner and draped them over her until he'd fashioned a gown, perhaps it was fitting that it was made of rags and tatters.

He stood up as the sounds from outside the room came to him, men's voices, horses being saddled, corral gates swinging open, and the thunder of hooves. He strained his ears and guessed there were some eight riders. He waited and let the sounds fade away before he went to the door. He wondered if Mexico Jack had left a guard outside. Probably not, he guessed. The man felt the room too sturdy to break out of and was secure in his smug arrogance. Yet he'd not take chances, Fargo told himself as he carefully put the key into the lock. He turned it slowly, heard the lock come open, and pushed the door open an inch, then another inch, and finally opened it wider as he saw no one waiting there.

He ran forward and paused at the entranceway to sweep the bunkhouse with a quick glance. Nothing moved and he ran again. He smiled when he saw they had left the Ovaro still saddled in the corral. But he swerved toward the bunkhouse as he suddenly realized he was completely unarmed. He stepped into the bunkhouse and moved from bunk to bunk in search of an extra rifle or six-gun. But he found nothing and stopped at the barn, settling for a pitchfork, which he carried in one hand as he sent the Ovaro from the corral. He picked up the hoofprints easily and followed at a steady pace, seeing that they were riding hard. They crossed the hills the way he had come but took another path at the far end. He followed and soon saw that they were riding to reach the Sunrise River. Suddenly one of the riders left the others and rode southwest.

Fargo halted, his lips pulled back. Then he turned and followed the tracks of the lone rider, unwilling to risk surprises. The tracks led over a hillock and he saw where the rider had halted to scan the terrain below before moving on. Fargo rode at the edge of a line of red cedar when he pulled into the trees. The rider was coming back and Fargo stayed hidden. He watched the man pass and turn into a narrow cut and gallop east. Cursing, Fargo followed the man and realized the rider had been sent to make sure the wagons hadn't turned off some-place. Angry at the lost time the diversion had cost him, he stayed back and followed the man until he rejoined the others.

Again, Fargo reined to a halt alongside a stand of junipers. The river gleamed in the sun and Fargo saw that the wagons had halted, Mexico Jack and his men surrounding them. Caroline had halted at the edge of the junipers, the second wagon with the big Percherons strung out behind her. Staying inside the trees, Fargo moved closer. There were six men beside Mexico Jack and Holly. They were spread out. Mexico Jack was closest to Caroline, and Holly and one of the men were a few steps behind her. Ben held a rifle raised to fire and Fargo drew closer, still inside the junipers. "Put it down, Ben," Fargo heard Caroline say.

"The senorita is very wise," Mexico Jack said.

"Don't hope that Fargo's going to come save you. He's under lock and key," Holly added. "But we'll talk about him later. We'll take the serum now."

At a gesture from Mexico Jack, two of the men moved toward Caroline's wagon. Holly, the other two men, and Mexico Jack also dismounted and one stood back from the others. Grateful for the junipers, Fargo moved within a few feet of the man who was apart from the others, his eyes on the gun in the man's holster. He had to get his hands on the weapon. Without it, he'd be but a helpless bystander. Even with it, he'd have no time to choose targets, he realized. He would have to empty the gun in a furious hail of bullets and hope for the best. He halted at the very edge of the juniper and raised the pitchfork as Mexico Jack stepped to Caroline, grasping her by the arm and pulling her from the wagon. "You, too," he ordered Ben. As the old driver swung to the ground, Mexico Jack smashed his head with a pistol butt and stepped back as Ben crumpled.

"You rotten bastard," Caroline flung at the man, and she started to kneel down to Ben when Mexico Jack caught her arm again and sent her sprawling.

"Watch your tongue, *mujer*," he snapped. Fargo's arm drew back. With Caroline and Ben on the ground, he wouldn't find a better moment. He flung the pitchfork and turned it into a three-pronged javelin as it sailed through the air. He was running and racing forward as the pitchfork left his hand so that he reached the man only seconds after the three sharp prongs hurtled into the back of the man's neck and shoulder blades. As the man screamed in pain and fell forward, Fargo was yanking the gun from his holster and rolling and coming up on one knee. The others turned in surprise as Fargo fired, swinging the gun from one side to the other, spraying a hail of bullets. There was no time to stop and pick targets, he knew, no time to aim, to indulge in pinpoint accuracy. He fired furiously and two figures doubled over as they fell, their abdomens spurting red.

Holly's face flashed in front of him as he continued to fire, her mouth falling open. Surprise flooded her face for an instant, then shock, and finally pain. The scarlet stain spread over her breasts as she pitched forward. She vanished from his sight as he swung the gun and pulled on the trigger and he saw another face twist in pain and a trickle of red bubble from contorted lips. Fargo heard the click of the hammer as it hit on an empty cartridge chamber and he flung himself forward, diving sideways as the shot hurtled over his head. As he rolled to the juniper he glimpsed the bodies that littered the ground in front of Caroline's wagon. He also glimpsed the lone remaining figure firing another shot at him as he ran forward on his ornate Mexican boots.

Crashing into the juniper, Fargo fought his way through a tangle of creosote brush, stayed low, and saw Mexico Jack coming into the trees after him. The man halted, half hidden behind a tree trunk. "You cannot hide, not in the juniper," he called and Fargo cursed the truth in the words. The juniper woods could be knotty and thick-branched but the foliage wasn't dense enough to offer real refuge. He'd never be able to hide there for long. "You are a surprising fellow, Fargo. I never expected to see you here. How did you do it?" Mexico Jack asked. The man was consumed with curiosity, that was real enough, but he wanted more from the question. He wanted a location, a spot to shoot. "You might as well tell me. You will not leave here alive. I will kill you with your own gun or cut you to ribbons with your own knife," the man said.

Fargo stayed silent and motionless. Turning the two choices in his mind, he decided his best chance would be the knife. It was really a devil's choice, he realized. The man had fired two shots from the Colt and had four left. Fargo's eyes went to the tangle of dried branches at his back. They were brittle. They'd snap, not entangle, and he gathered every muscle in his powerful legs. He'd give the man an answer he'd not comprehend and turn his second objective back on him. "Talk, Fargo. How did you do it?" Mexico Jack called.

"Melita sent me," Fargo said as he flung himself in a backward dive, crashing into the dry branches. But he counted on something else as he did. Mexico Jack fired the Colt but he was unaware of the gun's hair-trigger sensitivity. He grunted in grim satisfaction as the man's two shots were too fast and too high. "Four," he counted aloud as he rolled and came up on one knee beside a tree.

"*Roñoso,*" Mexico Jack snarled as he ran forward. Fargo rose and ran, darting between trees. The dryness of the woods made silence impossible and he glimpsed the man racing after him. He turned and stopped beside a tree and let Mexico Jack see him. The man fired instantly and again miscalculated the sensitivity of the Colt's trigger action as the shot went wide, plowing into a branch.

"Five," Fargo muttered as he darted forward again. He dropped into a crouch and plowed through an overhanging cluster of the sharp-pointed blue-gray needles. Reaching up, he seized a handful of the branchlets. He swung all his weight on them and tore them off as he fell to the ground. On his feet again, he saw Mexico Jack turn and follow him. He darted to the right, dropped to the ground, and lay still. The man charged, and coming closer, drew to a halt, his eyes sweeping the shrubby woods as he listened. Swinging his arm in a flat arc from his prone position, he flung the cluster of branchlets. They hit against others some dozen feet away and Mexico Jack spun, his pull on the trigger an automatic reaction. He tried to hold back but the Colt's delicacy refused to let him, and his shot plowed harmlessly into the brush. "Six," Fargo snapped and rose to his feet. He stepped into the clear and saw the man pull the double-edged knife from his belt.

A grin of anticipation touched the man's face as he came forward. "The knife, then. I will enjoy it more," he said, and Fargo moved sideways and felt the dry brush and fallen branches under his feet. It was no terrain for facing a knife, he realized. The footing made a slip at the wrong moment almost a certainty. He needed flat, open ground where he could turn and twist without being slowed or tripped. He moved backward, circling as he did, and Mexico Jack kept the grin on his face. He quickened his steps, came in faster, and Fargo retreated again, continuing in the half circle. He made no attempt to close with the man and saw arrogance as well as anticipation in the man's face.

Mexico Jack plainly thought he was retreating out of fear and Fargo grunted in satisfaction. Overconfidence was the Achilles heel of the arrogant. He kept backpedaling. Ducking under the low branches hung with dark brown cones, he circled again. The edge of the juniper cluster came into sight. He darted, with a quick burst of speed, and saw Mexico Jack come after him. The trees ended and Fargo ran into open land. The converted hay wagon and the brace of Percherons were only a dozen yards away. Fargo turned as Mexico Jack burst into the open, the razor-sharp blade held in front of him. The man advanced slowly, now, waving the blade tantalizingly. "It is a good blade. I like the feel of it," Mexico Jack said.

"Some folks call it an Arkansas toothpick. It throws real good," Fargo said.

Mexico Jack's smile was oily. "You'd like that, wouldn't you?" he said. "The chance of a miss? No, my friend, no more chances with you." His hand shot out, a short, upward thrust, and Fargo pulled his body backward, twisting away again as the man followed with a short, flat, slicing blow. Fargo felt the ground under his feet, firm and flat, with no branches to trip him and no dry brush to tangle around his ankles. But Mexico Jack enjoyed the same, he realized, and the man was quick. Fargo pulled away from another short, swiping blow. He tried to counter with a left to the head and missed as the man ducked away. A quick thrust of the knife had Fargo twisting away as he felt the blade brush his ribs. He danced away, giving ground again as the man pressed the attack with short, quick thrusts of the knife.

Fargo gathered his calf muscles, half leaped, and tried to close one hand around the man's wrist, but Mexico Jack ducked back, ramming the knife forward. Fargo sucked his stomach in as he twisted and heard the knife rip through his shirt. He lunged away, regained his balance, and saw Mexico Jack come at him again. This time he came forward with little dancing motions from left to right. Fargo tried feinting with him, but found that the man had a catlike quickness, the knife blows coming closer and closer. Ducking low, Fargo tried a looping left hook under one of the blows. He came up short and almost paid the price as a downward knife blow grazed his arm. He circled and came up with his back only inches away from the sides of the hay wagon.

Mexico Jack came at him and Fargo stayed in place, letting fear come into his eyes. He took another half step back, and was upset when his back touched the wagon. Mexico Jack rushed in, overconfidence letting him plunge the blade forward. Fargo counted off split seconds before he dropped to the ground and the man plunged the blade into the side of the wagon. Cursing, Mexico Jack yanked at the blade to pull it free. He had it almost out when Fargo's whistling left hook came up almost from the ground. It smashed into the man's jaw, knocking him backward and away from the wagon. Fargo followed with a right cross that landed high on the man's cheek as Mexico Jack tried to ruck away. Weaving out of a crouch, the man threw two fast blows that Fargo parried, trying to reach the knife still imbedded in the side of the wagon.

Fargo's blow sank into the pit of his stomach and Mexico Jack doubled over as a groan of pain burst from his lips. "That's for Doc Dodson," Fargo said as the man stayed doubled up for a long moment. When he rose, he tried a looping left that missed, and Fargo's blow smashed into his jaw. "That's for all those poor people in the Turner wagons," Fargo said. Mexico Jack staggered backward and fell against the wagon. He turned and reached out and closed his hand around the knife blade, somehow managing to pull it free. He tried to turn with the knife, but Fargo's blow, driven with the force of a ramrod, smashed deep into the small of his back. With a groan of pain, the man sank to his knees, his face against the side of the wagon. "That's for Caroline," Fargo said, closing one hand around the man's shirt collar and pulling him to his feet.

Finding a reserve of strength, Mexico Jack tore free of the grip, and the knife still in his hand, tried a slicing blow. Fargo leaped back and the knife grazed his chest. He shot a short, straight right that crashed into the man's jaw before he could bring the knife up again. Mexico Jack fell against the wagon. He tried to get away along the side of the wagon, but stumbled and fell forward as he reached the Percherons. He fought to his feet, his mouth hanging open as he gasped for breath. Fargo lifted a whistling left hook that turned the man almost around as it sent him falling. Mexico Jack crashed into the foreleg of one of the massive Percherons, his body twisting as he fell forward. Fargo's lips pulled back in a grimace as he saw the huge horse rise up on its hind legs. Startled, it pawed the air and then came down on its forelegs with all its weight.

He turned his face away, but he heard the sound of Mexico Jack's body being crushed, breastbone, collarbone, ribs, abdomen, and pelvis, and with it a terrible sound of bodily fluids being expelled as though a giant melon had been split open. "That was for Melita," Fargo murmured, his face still turned away. He walked away, and lips still pulled back, he heard a moan from Caroline's wagon and saw old Ben standing, holding a hand to the back of his head. He'd almost reached Ben when he saw the figure running from another patch of juniper. He stopped and let Caroline fling herself against him, arms clutched tightly around him.

"I saw him go into the woods after you. I ran to hide. I was so afraid," she said. He held her until she stopped trembling and led her back to where Ben had found a cold cloth for his head.

"It's over," he told her. "Finally over."

"A mission of mercy that never had a chance," Caroline said.

"We're bringing the serum back," he said. "It's something." He heard the weakness of his words, but he had nothing better to offer and he left her with Ben while he retrieved the Colt and his knife. Caroline drove as they started back and Fargo rode the Ovaro alongside her. She wrapped herself in silence and he let her hold to her own thoughts. When night came, she lay down beside him but only her hand touched his.

"I want to wait till we're back," she murmured. "Is that hard to understand?"

"No," he said. "When the moment's right everything else will be right." Her fingers closed around his and stayed there as she fell asleep. It was late afternoon when they reached Green Springs. When they drew up to the white frame house, he unloaded the serum and carried it into a cabinet inside the examination room.

"Sell the wagons and the horses. I suspect the Percherons will bring a handsome price," Caroline told Ben. "Whatever you get is yours. You deserve a bonus."

"Good luck to you both," Ben said as he drove the wagons away.

"Come back when you finish stabling the Ovaro," Caroline said. Fargo made arrangements for the horse and returned to the house to find Caroline waiting, clothed in a belted, dark blue robe. Night fell as she led him to her room, a spacious and comfortably furnished space, he noted, with a wide bed at one side.

"What will you do now?" he asked.

"Stay on. The town will need someone. It'll be a good while before another doctor arrives. Meanwhile, I can handle the ordinary things, pills, fevers, sore throats, bruises."

"And injections," he added.

"No," she said, and his brows lifted. "I'm going to leave injections to you," she said and pulling at the belt of the robe, the garment slipped from her. He stared, once again, at the delicate white porcelain teacup skin, the slightly shallow breasts with the nipples of faintest pink. But most of all, the pale-fire eyes again glowed with the colorless fire he had come to admire. She came to him and pressed the modest breasts against his face. "Deal?" she asked. "Over and over?"

"Definitely," he said. Pure mercy had been the start of it. Pure pleasure would be the finish. The world was made of trade-offs.

LOOKING FORWARD!
The following is the opening
section from the next novel in the exciting
Trailsman series from Signet:

THE TRAILSMAN #189
MISSOURI MASSACRE

1861—Missouri, the Show-Me State,
where those who let their guard
down are quickly shown how deadly
the frontier can be . . .

The anguished squeal of a horse in agony jarred Skye Fargo awake.

For most of that morning the Trailsman had been slowly winding his way westward along a rutted road that paralleled the Missouri River. The thick, muggy air, the buzzing drone of insects, and the gentle gurgle of the broad river had combined to make his eyelids as heavy as lead. Halfway between St. Louis and Jefferson City, he had taken to dozing in the saddle. He knew it was dangerous but he could not help himself.

Dangerous, because war was brewing. Several Southern states were on the verge of seceding from the Union. The issue of slavery was doing what the British and the rest of America's enemies had never been able to do. It was tearing the country apart.

Many feared that if Abraham Lincoln were to be elected president in the fall, war would break out.

Already, rival factions were often at each other's throats. Groups of armed men roamed at will. Homes were burned. Partisans on both sides had been brutally shot or hung.

To make matters worse, outlaw bands were taking advantage of the turmoil to plunder and rape and murder as they saw fit. Missouri was one of the states hardest hit by the violence.

It had become so bad that lone travelers took their lives in their hands. Going about after dark was discouraged. When men went anywhere, they went armed. And they regarded anyone they did not know with suspicion.

Fargo had never seen the like. A dozen times that morning he had come on fellow wayfarers. All of them had given him a wide berth while nervously fingering rifles or revolvers. Once a family in an open wagon had clattered past, heading east. Fargo had smiled and touched his hat brim. In response, the brawny farmer holding the reins had dropped a hand to a shotgun resting across his lap. The threat had been as plain as the farmer's scowl.

It was a shame, Fargo mused. The people of Missouri had always been so friendly, so kind.

The big man in buckskins was glad that in a few days he would reach Kansas City. There, he would treat himself to a couple of nights spent gambling in the company of a certain lusty dove he was fond of. Then he planned to strike off across the vast prairie to the Rockies.

Fargo had earned some time to himself. He had just delivered an urgent army dispatch from Denver to St.

Louis in record time. Days of grueling travel had left him exhausted from lack of sleep and gaunt from lack of food. His pinto stallion was no better off. The Ovaro plodded along with its head drooping, its tail limp.

That is, until those piercing whinnies rent the humid Missouri air. Both Fargo and his stallion were instantly alert.

Fargo's right hand automatically dropped to the Colt strapped to his right hip. His keen lake blue eyes probed the road and the green wall of vegetation that bordered it. A woman's scream eclipsed the squeals, punctuated by the crack of a gunshot that goaded him into applying his spurs just lightly enough to bring the pinto to a gallop.

Fresh ruts of a distinctive size and depth gave Fargo a clue to the source of the whinnies. He swept around two bends, reining up sharply as he went around the second. With good reason.

A stagecoach had come to an abrupt stop forty feet away. It had to, or else it would have crashed into a huge tree that lay sprawled across the road. As it was, the driver had not had enough time in which to react. He had tried to stop the team but momentum had carried the foremost pair into the obstacle. One horse was down, thrashing in a frenzy. The other reared, kicking at a limb that gouged its belly.

All this Fargo took in at a glance. Of more immediate interest was the stage and those who ringed it.

Perched on the seat was the driver, frozen in place with a hand pressed to a bloody shoulder. On the dusty ground beside the front wheel lay the motionless guard, bright scarlet stains creeping across the front of his shirt.

Those responsible had the stage hemmed in on either side. Five scruffy men wearing bandanas over the lower half of their faces, their hat brims pulled low, held leveled pistols.

A sixth gunman had dismounted and flung the door wide. He was gesturing for those inside to step out. An elderly woman appeared. Stepping back, he impatiently wagged his pistol. The terrified matron awkwardly climbed down, and was roundly cursed for being so slow.

So far Fargo was in luck. The racket the team was making had drowned out the thud of the Ovaro's hooves. And since he had halted before he was fully in the open, the bandits were unaware of his presence. He palmed his Colt but did not shoot. Not when the elderly woman might be caught by stray lead.

"Come on, damn your mangy hides!" the impatient gunman rasped. "We don't have all day!" He was a tall drink of water, his chin covered with stubble, a thick mustache framing his upper lip. His filthy clothes, a red flannel shirt, overalls, and a battered brown hat, were fit to be burned.

Next to emerge was a mouse of a man in a gray suit and bowler, a black valise clutched to his chest as if it contained precious gems. "What is the meaning of this outrage, sir?" he demanded in a mousy voice that perfectly matched his mousy features.

"Can't you guess, idiot?" growled the gunman. Grasping the front of the passenger's shirt, he yanked.

The mouse squeaked in fright as he was flung to the earth with such force he lost both the bowler and the black bag. To his credit, he was more mad than afraid, and he pushed up off the dirt, sputtering in fury. "How dare you! No one manhandles Mortimer J. Forbush! I'm a lawyer, and I'll see you thrown into prison until you rot!"

A couple of the mounted bandits cackled. One nodded at their apparent leader and said, "Better watch yourself, boss! That law wrangler is liable to bust your skull with one of those thick law books his kind tote everywhere!"

Their leader was not amused. Without warning, he kicked Forbush in the stomach, then snarled, "You have a leaky mouth, pilgrim." Bending, he snatched up the valise. "What's in this bag of yours, that you were hugging it to death? Money, maybe?"

"No! Don't!" Mortimer yelled, but he was in too much pain to prevent the outlaw from opening the valise and dumping the contents. A folder and dozens of sheets of paper fluttered to the ground. "Those are important documents!"

"Are they, now?" the gunman sneered. Hiking a boot, he was going to stomp on the pile when he realized another passenger was climbing down.

"Leave him be, you mean man"

A pint-sized wildcat tore into the leader, flailing at him with tiny fists and feet. It was a girl of ten or twelve, as fearless as she was rash. Her attack took the gunman and his companions by surprise. Stupefied, they gawked, then burst into rowdy mirth. Except for their leader. He gripped the girl's wrist and shook her as a coyote might shake a marmot it was about to devour.

"That's enough out of you, sprout! Behave or I'll turn you over my knee!" So saying, the gunman flung her down next to the lawyer. But she bounced right back up and would have torn into him again had Mortimer J. Forbush not snagged her ankle.

"My ma used to say that only yellow dogs pick on women and kids! What does that make you, mister?"

A bearded bear on a roan slapped his thigh and hollered, "She sure is a hellion, Krill. Careful, or she might whup you!"

The leader stiffened and glared. So did some of the other outlaws. The bear on the roan, suddenly aware of his mistake, flushed and declared, "Damnation! Me and my big mouth. Now what do we do?"

"What do you think, stupid?" Krill shot back.

"But she's so young and pretty," the bear said sullenly. "It goes against my grain to make wolf meat of children."

Krill had a sharp retort on the tip of his tongue, but just then another figure stepped from the stage and he spun, raising his six-gun. His open mouth yawned wider, as did his eyes. All the cutthroats, in fact, were so dazzled by the figure that they gasped in brutish amazement, tinged with rising lust.

Fargo had seen the woman before they did. She was dressed in a fine, full dress that could not conceal the shapely swell of her bosom or the tantalizing curve of her slender hips and legs. Burnished brown hair was held up in a fashionable bun, revealing a smooth neck and rounded shoulders. Her face was exquisite. Cherry lips curled in defiance. Blue eyes blazed disdain. Her nose would have done justice to a statue sculpted by a master sculptor. High cheeks and a square chin hinted at inner strength.

"You will not lay a finger on that girl, or on any of

us," the vision of loveliness stated. Moving to the child's side, she draped a protective arm over the girl's shoulders. "Rob us and go, Bart Krill."

The leader was taken aback by her defiance. "How do you know who I am?" he blurted.

The woman sniffed. "Oh, come now. Everyone in these parts has heard of you. For four years you have preyed on innocents like ourselves. You've stopped stages, waylaid merchants, even attacked settlers in their houses." Her chin jutted forward. "You are vermin, Bart Krill. As vile as any man who ever drew breath."

More laughter rumbled from the bear on the roan. He found humor in everything, it seemed. "Hear that, Krill?" he taunted. "You're so famous, we might as well not bother covering our faces anymore."

"Shut up, Barstow!" Krill fumed. Jabbing his revolver at the beauty, he snarled, "Since you know so much about me, Miss-High-and-Mighty, you know what to expect before we're through, don't you?"

At that the woman blanched and firmed her grip on the child. The lawyer had risen to his knees and was collecting his documents. Raw terror riveted the elderly woman where she had stopped.

Fargo cocked his Colt. He was anxious to do something, but any move he made would put the lives of the passengers in peril. If only the gunmen would lower their pistols! He saw Krill stalk to the stage and glower at the driver.

"Throw down the box, and be quick about it!" The outlaw had the look of a rabid wolf about to pounce. It would not take much to set him off.

Meekly, the driver complied. A middle-aged man, he

was smart enough not to do anything that would cause Krill's trigger finger to tighten. Grunting, he hoisted the heavy metal strongbox out of the front boot and onto the lip of the seat. Pausing to balance himself, he pushed, and the strongbox thudded at Krill's feet.

The outlaw turned the box over and swore bitterly at finding a padlock as big as his hand. "What the hell is this?" he demanded. "I've never seen one this size before."

"It's the owner's idea," the driver said. "To make it harder for anyone who has no business opening the box."

"Is that so?" Krill said angrily, and like a striking rattler he pivoted and put a slug in the driver's torso. At the blast, the elderly woman screamed. The driver's hand flew to his sternum, he tried to speak but failed, then he pitched from the seat to wind up in a disjointed heap next to the express guard.

"You beast!" cried the woman, who was shielding the girl. "I hope they catch you and hang you for this!"

Krill turned and leered at her. "If they do, you won't be around to see it, bitch." Motioning at two of his men, he barked, "Get off those nags and unhitch the team. I want the strongbox tied onto one of the horses. We'll open it later, once we're in the clear."

As the pair swung down, Fargo edged the Ovaro forward. He was upset with himself. Had he acted sooner, the driver would still be alive. The passengers would soon share the poor man's fate unless he did something right away.

Bart Krill faced them. Hitching at his belt, he swaggered toward the woman, his features a wicked mask of sadistic evil. "What's your name, sister?"

"Why do you want to know?" she said.

Again Krill struck, this time lashing out with the back of a hand that caught the woman full on the cheek and staggered her. The little girl leaped to the woman's defense but she was swatted aside as casually as if she were a fly. She collided with the lawyer, who kept her from falling. The elderly matron recoiled in horror.

Fargo tensed. The pair unhitching the team had holstered their hardware. Barstow and the remaining two were watching Krill's antics. All but Barstow had lowered their pistols. He would never have a better chance.

"Bethany Cole, as if it's any of your business," the beauty revealed. She had no choice. Krill had elevated a fist to hit her again. "I teach school in Jefferson City. My brother is a deputy there. He will hunt you to the ends of the world if you so much as lay a finger on me."

Krill snickered. "Oh, I aim to do more than poke you with my *finger.*" He gloated at her, and hungrily ogled her lush body. "So what if your kin is a lawdog? We've had more posses on our tail than a coon dog has fleas, and they ain't caught us yet. I reckon your brother won't be any luckier than they were." Brazenly, he extended a grimy hand toward her breasts. "Let's see if that's all you in there."

"Don't you dare!" Bethany cried, swatting his arm. "I'd rather die than let you have your way."

With a flick of both ankles, Skye Fargo spurred the stallion into a gallop and swept into the open. He banged a shot at one of the mounted outlaws, who snapped in his direction. The man dropped like a stone. Immediately, Fargo aimed at Bart Krill, thinking he had the killer dead to rights, but Krill was craftier than he gave the man credit for being, and unbelievably fast. In a bound Krill reached the schoolmarm, clamped a forearm around her throat, and shoved her in front of him, using her as a living shield.

Fargo veered into the growth on the left side of the road as pistols cracked and lead buzzed around him. He answered but did not score. A tree trunk he passed was smacked by a slug. The tip of a branch was clipped off above him. Reigning up, he fired at one of the bandits who had been unhitching the team. The bullet caught the man in the leg just as he climbed onto his horse. Slumping over the saddle, the outlaw goaded the animal into racing off down the road.

Bart Krill was backing toward his own mount. Bethany Cole struggled mightily, but Krill's whipcord frame harbored sinews of steel. He reached his horse and paused to bellow, "The strongbox! Someone get the damn strongbox!"

But the rest of the hardcases were more interested in saving their own carcasses. The other man who had been working on the team was already astride a dun and racing pell-mell eastward. Another killer joined him. That left Barstow to cover Krill as the latter prepared to fork leather.

"Hurry up!" Barstow thundered, firing at random. "I can't see where the *hombre* went."

Krill cast a last longing glance at the strongbox, then shoved the teacher and vaulted onto his bay. "Bunch of cowards!" he raged.

Fargo wanted to stop the butcher at all costs. Streaking toward the road, he squeezed off a shot at the very split-second that Krill wheeled the bay. His shot missed. Barstow came to Krill's aid, shooting twice. One of the leaden hornets clipped Fargo's hat. Bending low over the saddle, Fargo slanted to the right to put a thicket between them. When he straightened, Krill and the big bear were skirting the downed tree. Both sent lead into the vegetation to pin him down long enough for them to gain the straight stretch beyond.

Fargo raced in pursuit. Breaking from cover near the stagecoach, he reined toward the tree, only to be brought to a halt by a shout from Bethany Cole. "Stop! Please! Don't leave us!"

She had regained her feet. The elderly matron had broken into tears and was being comforted by the lawyer, while the little girl was staring in mute dismay at the body of the driver.

For a few moments Fargo wavered, torn between trying to bring an end to Krill's reign of terror and doing what he could for the passengers. It was the child who made up his mind for him. Running to the driver, she knelt and placed a hand on the man's forehead.

"Miss Cole! Mr. Forbush! Come here! I think Mr. Weaver is still alive!"

Reluctantly, Fargo watched the fleeing outlaws vanish around a bend. If the girl was right, going after them was out of the question. An innocent man's life was at stake. Jumping down, he dashed to the driver.

Weaver's eyes were open, mirroring great torment. Gasping in agony, he said, "I hurt! Oh God, how I hurt!"

"We have to get him to a doctor," Bethany Cole declared.

Which was easier said than done, Fargo mused. They could not go anywhere with that massive tree blocking the road. "Tend him as best you can," he told the school-marm, then hurried to the team. The stricken horse was back on its feet and acting none the worse for its ordeal.

After making sure the traces and harness on all six animals were secure, Fargo unhitched the team by separating the tongue from the coach. It took some doing, but he soon had them turned around. Now came the hard part. Using his lariat and a rope taken from the horse of the outlaw he had slain, he tied several loops around the maple and made the other ends hold fast to the wagon tongue.

Picking up the reins, Fargo let out with a whoop and flicked them at the horses. Automatically the team surged forward, but they were brought up short. Fargo urged them on, pitting their powerful bodies against the immense weight of the tree. Again and again he whipped the rear animals. Again and again the whole team threw itself into the effort.

At first nothing happened. Fargo was beginning to think the maple was too heavy. A grating sound convinced him to the contrary. Inch by gradual inch, the tree slid from its resting place, angling toward the south side of the road. By holding to the border and carefully gauging the angle, Fargo dragged the upper end far enough off the road to permit the stage to get by.

Undoing the ropes, Fargo turned the team a second time. Once he had aligned the tongue with the rod shafts, it was a simple matter to reattach it. They were ready to go. Or almost. He tied the Ovaro to the rear, set his

Henry up on the driver's seat, and replaced the strong-box in the front boot.

Weaver was unconscious but breathing. Bethany Cole held one of his callused hands, the little girl the other. She looked up at Fargo, revealing eyes the same color as his own.

"Stand back," Fargo directed. Stooping, he gently lifted the older man and eased Weaver onto the floor of the coach. A folded blanket on the right seat sufficed as a pillow. It was the best they could do, under the circumstances. "Climb in and hold on tight," he advised. "You're in for the ride of your lives."

They recognized the urgency. Even the child clambered swiftly back inside without comment, and Fargo slammed the door. As he placed a foot on the hub of the front wheel and reached up to grasp the rail that framed the driver's box, the lawyer stuck his head out the window.

"What about the holdup man you shot, stranger? And the express messenger? Surely we're not going to let them lie there for scavengers to eat?"

Fargo frowned. Leave it to a lawyer to nitpick when every moment they wasted was critical. "You can stay here until help comes, if you want, and shoo the buzzards and coyotes away."

"By *myself*?" Forbush said. "Why, Krill might return. Or wolves might show up. Or—"

"Figures," Fargo muttered, pulling himself up. In short order he leaned the Henry against his leg, worked the brake lever, hefted the whip a few times, and lumbered the team into motion with a sharp crack of the lash over their heads.

The Central Overland stage swayed as Fargo moved into the middle of the road. He had handled Concords before, but never under these circumstances. Over eight feet high and weighing more than a ton, they had the ungainly aspect of overfed geese. Thanks to their ingenious design, though, which suspended the carriage on thoroughbraces made of three-inch-thick strips of leather, riding in one was like riding in a cradle on wheels. Sturdily built, they took any abuse.

Fargo proved that. He pushed the six horses to their limit, taking turns at breakneck speed. Several times the coach leaned so far to either side that the inner wheels spurned the ground. When the going was straight, he fairly flew, heedless of ruts, holes, and dips. The stage jounced and bounced and creaked and rattled. Twice the lawyer called out, upset, but Fargo ignored the protests.

Never for a moment did Fargo think of stopping to rest. He roared like a lion at anyone who blundered into his path. Some people shook their fists and hurled oaths, but he did not care.

In the middle of the hot afternoon the stage rumbled into Jefferson City. Fargo had been there before. So he had no trouble locating the Holladay Overland Mail Express Company. Bringing the sweat-lathered team to a halt right in front of it, he yelled, "The stage was held up! We need help!"

As usual, a crowd was on hand. They thronged around the Concord. Company officials whisked Weaver into the office and sent for a doctor and the town marshal.

In all the confusion and excitement, Fargo was largely forgotten. He walked to the rear boot, untied the Ovaro, and was about to slip quietly off when someone tugged on his elbow.

"Hold on there, stranger," Mortimer J. Forbush said. Beside him was the little girl. Behind him stood the schoolmarm and the matron. "None of us have thanked you properly for saving our lives."

"No need," Fargo said. He was tired and sore and hungry enough to eat a buffalo raw. A hot bath, a thick steak, and half a bottle of whiskey, and he would feel like a whole man again. Nodding to the ladies, he prepared to depart.

"What's your name, sir, if you don't mind my asking?" Bethany politely inquired.

"Skye Fargo, ma'am."

Suddenly the lawyer became as rigid as a fireplace poker. "It can't be!" he exclaimed. "After all this time! To meet you like this!"

"What are you jabbering about?" Fargo asked, then saw the child. She wore a peculiar expression, and she gulped air as if she had something stuck in her throat. "Are you all right, little one?" he asked, perplexed.

Throwing her arms wide, the girl clasped his legs and clung to him as if afraid he would try to run off. "We've found you! At long last!"

"What's this all about?" Fargo said. "Why are you acting this way?"

The girl pulled back. "Don't you know?" Her next words startled him to his core. "You're my *pa!*"

WHISPERS OF THE MOUNTAIN
BY TOM HRON

The Indians of Alaska gave the name Denali to the great sacred mountain they said would protect them from anyone who tried to take the vast wilderness from them. But now white men had come to Denali, looking for the vast lode of gold that legend said was hidden on its heights. A shaman lay dead at the hands of a greed-mad murderer, his wife was captive to this human monster, and his little daughter braved the frozen wasteland to seek help. What she found was lawman Eli Bonnet, who dealt out justice with his gun, and Hannah, a woman as savvy a survivor as any man. Now in the deadly depth of winter, a new hunt began on the treacherous slopes of Denali—not for gold but for the most dangerous game of all....

from SIGNET

Prices slightly higher in Canada.   (0-451-187946—$5.99)

EAGLE
by Don Bendell

Chris Colt didn't believe in the legendary Sasquatch, no matter if witnesses told of a monstrously huge figure who slew victims with hideous strength and vanished like smoke in the air. But now in the wild Sangre de Cristo mountains of Colorado, even Chris Colt, the famed Chief of Scouts, felt a tremor of unease in his trigger finger. The horrifying murderer he was hunting was more brutal than any beast he had ever heard of, and more brilliant than any man he had ever had to best. Colt was facing the ultimate test of his own strength, skill, and savvy against an almost inhuman creature whose lethal lust had turned the vast unspoiled wilderness into an endless killing field. A creature who called himself—Eagle. . . .

from **SIGNET**